Danger in the Greenwood Tunnel

A Mason Twins Adventure

Alan Carter Thompson

DEDICATION

To my children,
Emily, Stephen, and Sara
who continue to keep a spirit of
adventure alive in me.

CONTENTS

CHAPTER 1: SCOUTING MISSION

"Mom is going to kill us!" Thomas always was the worry wart, and today was no exception.

"Relax, Shadow. After all, we're just working on our school project," said Joel.

The twin brothers rode their bikes up the rough path through the woods. Exposed roots on the path made the ride bumpy and small trees growing along the path extended thin leafy branches that occasionally smacked them in the face.

Thomas got nervous every time they took this shortcut. All he could think about was the old farm that they would have to cut across to get where they were going, and the "wild man" who lived there.

On the other hand, Joel was always fearless. How could twin brothers be so different? Joel thrived on adventure. Thomas preferred to play it safe. And Thomas could always tell when Joel was about to drag him off on some new adventure. Joel would start using their "code names." When Joel started calling himself "Vanguard," and calling Thomas "Shadow," Thomas knew the trouble was about to start.

As they reached the top of the hill, the old farm stretched out in front of them. The boys hopped off their bikes and rested them against a tree. Joel knelt down behind an old stump at the edge of the woods, and pulled out his plastic binoculars. "No sign of the enemy," he said. Just to be on the safe side, Thomas searched the horizon himself. There was no telling who or what might be in that run-down barn with the rusty metal roof. A thin wisp of smoke trailed away from the farm house chimney, warning them that the wild man was still alive and well. And the old dusty pickup truck parked in the dirt driveway told them that he was probably at home.

Thomas stared at each window of the weathered old white house, looking for that long gray beard and those fiery eyes. He had only seen the man up-close once in his life. It was the day the two brothers went to buy some climbing rope at the hardware store. When they stepped out of the door they nearly ran into the old man. His long beard and frizzy hair nearly hid his face, except for those fiery eyes. It was like running into a crazy-eyed wild beast. The encounter scared them so badly that they took off running for home—totally forgetting that they had ridden their bicycles to the store. They waited almost an hour before going back to get them.

Now, lowering his plastic binoculars, Joel spoke as if he was talking over a radio: "Shadow, this is Vanguard. The coast is clear. I repeat, the coast is clear."

"I hear you, Vanguard," Thomas said, feeling silly since his brother was only two feet away. "Ready when you are."

"Go!" Joel said, and the two brothers took off across the overgrown field like a cat with its tail on fire. By the wobbly barn, behind the long woodpile, over the fence, across the pasture, slowing down to climb through the barbed wire, the boys crossed the wild man's farm. As far as they could tell, only a couple of cows noticed their presence.

Out of sight now, they slowed down.

"We could have just looked it up in a book," Thomas said, still panting. Every year the 5th grade classes at Crozet Elementary School took on this local history assignment. They had to prepare a research project on the Greenwood Tunnel, an old train tunnel which cut through the mountain a few miles from the town of Crozet, Virginia. Thomas was right—there was plenty of information available back at school. The school library had books on local history and on the life and work of Claudius Crozet. Crozet was a French-born engineer who planned the four tunnels cutting through the Blue Ridge Mountains. He supervised the construction of these tunnels, including the Greenwood Tunnel, in the mid-1800s. But Joel wasn't satisfied to read about a tunnel he could go see for himself.

Down the hill, through the tall grass,

they bounded toward the railroad tracks. The two boys peered down the rails in both directions. The tracks stretched out before them, disappearing around a curve to the east and stretching to the horizon to the west. But there was no tunnel in sight.

"Ms. Cox said the tunnel isn't used anymore," Thomas reminded his brother.

"Ten-four, Shadow," Joel said in a loud whisper. "Our mission is to find that tunnel, wherever it is."

They set out toward the west, with the sun in their eyes. It was late afternoon and time was running out. If they weren't home soon, they'd have major explaining to do.

Joel stopped suddenly. "Unidentified object at one o'clock!" he said, raising his plastic binoculars for a look. The tall structure cut into the hillside by the tracks. It was partially hidden by small trees and brush, but the gray concrete and red bricks stood out against the greens and browns of the surrounding growth. When they saw the tall stone archway, they knew they had found it.

Making their way through the brush, they approached the tunnel entrance. The entrance was sealed off now. The red brick archway was filled with a wall of white cement. Large gray cement columns stood on either side of the entrance, providing support for the structure. High on the wall was a round opening about fifteen inches across. It looked like some kind of air vent. Strangely, the leaves of the ivy growing at the edge of the vent were moving back and forth, even though no breeze was blowing.

Thomas looked at his watch nervously. "Come on, Joel, it's getting late." His brother ignored his plea and he knew why. He tried a different approach. "Vanguard, this is Shadow. It's time to head back."

"Ten-four, Shadow," Joel replied. Then, speaking into his own watch as if it were a radio, he said, "Home base, this is Vanguard. We have located the target and will return later for further exploration."

"That's what I'm afraid of," Thomas thought to himself.

* * * * *

"Where have you two been?" their mother asked. "It's almost supper time."

"We've been working on a school project," Joel answered. "The whole fifth grade is doing it, so we wanted to get a head start on everyone else."

"Well, get cleaned up so you can set the table," their mother said. "Your father has a meeting tonight so we can't be late."

Joel and Thomas Mason had moved to the Crozet area just two years back. Their father, the Reverend Rick Mason, was pastor of the Crozet Community Church. Two years earlier, they had been living in New Kent County, Virginia, over 100 miles to the east. The land in New Kent County was flat. So the hills and mountains of the Crozet area were a new experience for the Mason twins. When the people at Crozet Community Church had asked Rev. Mason to consider coming to be their pastor, he and his wife, Deanna, had wrestled with the decision of moving. When they decided to accept the invitation, they had hoped and prayed their sons would adjust quickly to their new home.

At the supper table, Thomas tried to keep the conversation away from their afternoon adventure. "So, Dad, what meeting do you have tonight?" he asked.

"The finance committee," their father replied. "We're planning to set up a food pantry in the church to help people who need food, so we need to plan for the expenses of setting up the pantry and buying some of the food we'll be giving away." Turning the conversation, he asked, "So what happened at school today?"

"We started a big school project today," Joel said.

Thomas panicked. This was just what he did *not* want to discuss with Mom and Dad. What if Mom asked what they had done this afternoon?

"Dad, do you know anything about the old train tunnel near here?" Joel asked.

"Do you mean the Greenwood Tunnel designed by Claudius Crozet?" his father asked. Joel nodded. "Well," his father continued, "when we first moved here, I did read a little about the area. That's just one of four tunnels that Crozet cut through the mountain. The longest one is the Blue Ridge Tunnel. It's over 4000 feet long. But those tunnels aren't used anymore."

"Why did they quit using it?" Thomas asked. If Joel insisted on discussing the subject, he might as well participate.

"Well, I think they became concerned about cave-ins." Rev. Mason replied. "The tunnel wasn't designed for the more powerful trains that came later."

"Is it caved in now?" asked Joel.

"Well, now, I can't say for sure," their father said. "But since I didn't read about any cave-ins, I suspect that the tunnel was intact when it was sealed up. I can tell you who might know. I have a friend who is a pastor now, but he used to be a railroad conductor. He has mentioned several times how he used to ride the train through this area. His name is Frank Stallings. Old Frank must have told me ten times about looking out of the train window and seeing the ripe peaches on the trees at Carter's farm each fall. Mr. and Mrs. Carter are members of our church who live by the train tracks near the Greenwood Tunnel. After work Frank would ride back up here and ask her if he could pick a few. I know he wouldn't mind telling you what he knows about the tunnel. And the Carters have already told us to bring you boys over to their farm sometime. So they'd love to talk with you about the trains that came by their farm, and the old tunnel."

The conversation turned to other topics, and both boys got a second helping of their mother's special meatloaf. It was one of their favorites.

After supper, Rev. Mason headed off to his meeting and the boys cleared the table. When they finished, they went to their rooms to finish their homework and listen to music. Bedtime came soon. Joel dreamed of the wonderful sights he imagined were waiting to be found inside the old abandoned tunnel. Thomas dreamed about getting caught by the wild man and being locked up in his rickety old barn.

CHAPTER 2: EVASIVE MANEUVERS

Their bus had just turned into the school driveway. Joel leaned across the aisle and said in a loud whisper, "Vanguard to Shadow—time for Escape Plan B." That could only mean one thing: Sherry West and Janice Taylor were waiting for Joel and Thomas, their "boyfriends," at the school entrance. Sherry had decided that she liked Thomas and Janice had decided that she liked Joel last year when they were in the same fourth grade class. By Thanksgiving, the boys were having to plan escape routes to avoid these persistent female admirers.

Things hadn't changed over the summer. Now, even though the twin boys were in a different fifth grade class from Sherry and Janice, the girls were still "madly in love" with Thomas and Joel.

This was serious business, so Thomas responded quickly, "Affirmative, Vanguard. Preparing for Escape Plan B."

When the squealing brakes of the bus brought them to a stop, the children gathered their belongings and exited the bus. Joel and Thomas slipped in behind Kevin Freeman, the biggest kid on the bus. As they hit the sidewalk, they ducked down behind Kevin and slipped behind the big evergreen bush by the sidewalk.

As Janice and Sherry searched through the mob of entering students for their "sweethearts," Thomas and Joel worked their way, from bush to bush, to the side of the building and through the double doors at the end of the hallway. As they moved quickly down the long hall toward their homeroom, they kept their eyes pointed toward the main entrance.

Five seconds later, the two girls appeared, moving toward them as fast as they could without actually running. Joel and Thomas picked up the pace and reached the door to their classroom with the girls less than ten feet away. Pretending not to see the girls, the twins ducked into the room and dashed behind a storage cabinet. Excited and still breathing hard, this time it was Thomas who whispered first: "Shadow to Vanguard—Mission accomplished."

Ms. Cox smiled as Thomas and Joel took their seats. This was only her second year as a teacher. She was the youngest and newest teacher at Crozet

Elementary, but she loved kids and knew a lot about them. She had been watching the "cat and mouse" game that Thomas and Joel had been playing with Sherry and Janice since the first day of school. When Ms. Cox saw the two girls standing outside the classroom door staring and smiling at the Mason twins, she decided to have a little fun herself.

"Thomas, Joel, could you do me a favor?" she asked.

Joel spoke up first, "Sure, Ms. Cox!" Thomas and Joel really liked Ms. Cox. In fact, they had a crush on their pretty young teacher. They would have done anything for her.

"Could you two boys put up these posters outside the door?" Ms. Cox had made posters showing some of the work that her students had done. The students had written poetry and illustrated their work. Ms. Cox was so proud of the accomplishments of her students that she liked for the principal, other teachers and students, and visiting parents to see their work, too. She also knew that the boys had managed to slip past the two girls that morning. Now they would be stuck out there with them for the next several minutes. "Take your time and make it look nice," Ms. Cox said with a sneaky grin.

When Thomas and Joel picked up the posters and headed for the door, they saw the two waiting girls' eyes light up. The boys' sassy grins turned into expressions of shock. "Escape Plan B" had just been out-foxed by "Teacher's Plan C." Ms. Cox winked at Sherry and Janice and called to them through the open doorway, "Could you two girls give Joel and Thomas a hand with those posters?"

It was a long three minutes for Joel and Thomas before the first bell rang and

Janice and Sherry had to head to their own homerooms. The twins had no idea that Ms. Cox knew *exactly* what she was doing when she sent them out there. They knew Ms. Cox was smart, fun, and sweet, but they had no idea how sneaky she was.

After recovering from the shock of his teacher's tricky assignment, Joel was eager to get back to their history project—the old railroad tunnel at Greenwood. His curiosity had been working overtime, and he had a long list of questions to ask and answers to find. Was there a way to get inside the tunnel? What was it like in there now? Had it caved in? Were there still train tracks inside? Joel could imagine turning the old tunnel into his own secret fort, where they could sit around and tell scary stories in the dark. He imagined building a go-cart that would zoom down the abandoned train tracks, with a big flashlight on the front to light the way. He imagined discovering some kind of hidden treasure—a bag of money left long ago by a bank robber who didn't know they would be sealing up the tunnel before he could return.

But he would have to wait, because math and science came first today. History wouldn't come until after lunch.

"What do *you* think, Joel?" Ms. Cox asked. Joel looked around to see every eye staring his way. He was so busy daydreaming that he didn't know what the question was. He wasn't even sure he knew what subject they were studying. All he had on his desk was a piece of paper with sketches of his train tunnel go-cart.

"Could you repeat the question?" Joel asked.

"We're on page 47 in the science

textbook, Joel." Ms. Cox was clearly upset that Joel had not been paying attention. She loved her children, and because of that she also had high expectations for them. Two of her expectations were that students would pay attention in class and do their very best. "Does anyone have an idea?" Ms. Cox asked.

Thomas, trying to restore the family honor, raised his hand quickly. When the teacher nodded, he blurted out, "I think you can tell how far away lightning is by measuring how long it takes for the sound to get to you." Thomas loved getting good grades and took his school work much more seriously than Joel did.

"Yes. Very good, Thomas," Ms. Cox said. "Now, sound travels through the air at about 1000 feet per second," she said, writing the numbers on the board. "And there are just over 5000 feet in a mile.

So, suppose you saw the flash of lightning, and you heard the thunder five seconds later. About how far away would the lightning be?"

"One mile!" yelled out Jackie Davis— "Wacky Jackie" they called her. Her hair was thick and frizzy and on bad days it stuck out all over. One day in the fourth grade, when she still had her old glasses with the thick frames, one of the other children thought she looked a little like a Mad Scientist, so he nicknamed her "Wacky Jackie." She did have a funny sense of humor that matched her nickname, and, while none of the boys would have admitted it, she was cute, too.

Wacky Jackie was often the first one to answer math questions and she was always the first to finish a page of math problems. Thomas admired her for being able to work problems in her head so fast, and sometimes he caught himself staring at her pretty face for reasons he himself didn't even understand.

"That's very good, Jackie," said Ms. Cox.

"Ms. Cox, Ms. Cox," called one student with his hand waving frantically.

"Yes, J.L.?"

With his hand still held high, J.L. said, "On the fourth of July we can see the fireworks show at the park from our front yard. When they explode, I always count 'chimpanzees' until I hear the 'boom.'"

A couple of the kids looked at him with puzzled expressions, wondering where he saw chimpanzees on the fourth of July.

"You know," J.L. said, "I count 'one chimpanzee, two chimpanzees, three chimpanzees.'"

Now those other kids knew he was crazy. Could it be that J.L. didn't know the difference between the fourth of July and the circus?

Seeing their confusion, and knowing what J.L. meant, Ms. Cox explained. "Class, some people use that as a way to measure seconds. It takes about one second to say the words 'one chimpanzee.' So, J.L., how high can you count before you hear the sound of the fireworks?"

"I always hear it at six chimpanzees," J.L. replied.

"So, class, does J.L. live *more* than a mile or *less* than a mile from the park?" the teacher asked.

"More!" they shouted, with Wacky Jackie's voice the first to be heard.

"Very good, class. Today when we go outside we'll be doing some experiments with sound. And tonight for homework I want you to read the section on pages 49 and 50. Since it's the weekend, I won't give you any written work, but I do want you to find out something. You know that sound travels through air. But what else does sound travel through? I'll expect you to have lots of answers for me Monday morning."

As Ms. Cox was finishing up the lesson on sound waves, the smell of fresh-made rolls had filled the hallways and crept into the classrooms. And the sound of growling stomachs was moving through the air at about 1000 feet per second. So her students were more than ready to put away their books and line up for the cafeteria.

At lunch, Joel began talking about his plans to revisit the old train tunnel. "Tomorrow is the perfect time for Operation Doorway. Since it's Saturday morning we'll have all the time we need to try and find a way into the tunnel. I'll pack all the equipment tonight."

"Right," Thomas said, wondering what in the world Joel meant by "equipment." He was really hoping that Joel wouldn't pack a bunch of stuff and then expect him to carry it. Maybe "equipment" meant a couple of canned lemonades and some of Mom's special Rice Krispie treats with M&Ms mixed in. Not likely, but he could always hope. "What are we going to tell Dad and Mom when they ask where we're going?"

"The truth, of course!" said Joel. "We're going to do research on our school project."

In Joel's mind, it was just that easy. But Thomas could think of a dozen ways that this whole adventure could turn into a giant disaster—a dozen ways they could end up in big trouble.

CHAPTER 3: RESEARCH

"OK, class, let's get quiet," Ms. Cox said. The students were still busy chattering as they returned to class after lunch. "It's time to work on your history research project. Today I want you to work in your small groups and use the research materials on the table by the window." Ms. Cox, with the help of the school librarian, had gathered lots of books and articles about Claudius Crozet and the Greenwood Tunnel.

Thomas and Joel picked up a few books from the table and went back to their desks to work. Thomas began making notes about Claudius Crozet's life, and the events that led up to the construction of the nearby tunnel. Joel searched through the words and pictures looking for just one thing: a way into that abandoned tunnel.

After a half hour of work, and trading books back and forth, Thomas and most of the other children had gotten a lot of information for their reports. Joel, after not finding a way into the tunnel, had gone back to daydreaming and doodling.

Thomas was perturbed that Joel was leaving all the research up to him. "If you're not going to help write the report, you could at least start working on the poster," Thomas said to Joel. In addition to the written report, each team had to put together a visual presentation—something they could show to the class when they gave their oral report. Joel was supposed to be making the headlines for the poster: "The Greenwood Tunnel, by Joel and Thomas Mason, Teacher: Ms. Cox, Room 14." But the thirty minutes had passed and Joel had only succeeded in drawing a new and improved model of his train tunnel go-cart.

"That's all the time we have for today, class," Ms. Cox announced. "Put all the materials back on the table and clean off your desks. It's time for Physical Education."

"That's just great," thought Thomas. "I'm the only one doing any real work on this project. Next time I'm going to ask the teacher to put me with Wacky Jackie. At least she would do her share of the work."

* * * * *

The rest of the school day flew by. Soon Joel and Thomas were back at home. Joel flew through the house, threw his school backpack in the closet, and grabbed his old camouflage backpack. Joel had gotten the backpack as part of an "outdoor adventure pack." It included a camouflage-covered sleeping bag and backpack, with matching binoculars—the same binoculars he used for their first trip to find the old train tunnel. Joel began filling the backpack with items for tomorrow's Operation Doorway.

Meanwhile Thomas stopped to talk with his mother in the kitchen. "Do you boys have any homework this weekend?" she asked.

"Just some science reading," Thomas replied, and seeing the opportunity he added, "And Joel has to get the poster started for our class history project. He's way behind."

"Well, go ahead and get as much as possible done before supper," Mrs. Mason said.

Thomas made his way back to his bedroom. His own room—at least this was one thing he didn't have to share with Joel. He could hear a sound through the wall that sounded like two squirrels wrestling in a cardboard box. Peeking into Joel's room, he saw two legs hanging out of the closet. "What are you doing?" Thomas asked.

The noise stopped and Joel slowly peeked out of the closet. "Shhhh!" he said in a whisper. "I'm gathering the equipment for tomorrow's mission— Operation Doorway."

"Don't bother whispering now," said Thomas. "Anyone who couldn't hear you bumping around in the closet is probably deaf anyway." Then, changing the subject, Thomas said, "Mom said you have to work on our school project now." With Mom's authority behind him, maybe now he could get Joel to pull his share of the load. "You're supposed to make the big titles for the poster. Here's the list."

Joel got up with a sigh, took the list, and headed off to the computer in the family room. Sometimes he got frustrated with Thomas, but Joel rarely got angry about anything. He figured that the sooner he finished the titles, the sooner he could finish preparing for tomorrow's adventure.

Joel typed up the titles, printed them out, and then took everything to the kitchen table. There he started filling in the letters with colored markers. While he was at it, he couldn't resist drawing a picture of the way the sealed-up tunnel entrance looked now. He tried to make it look extra spooky to catch the attention of the other kids in class. Joel couldn't wait until Operation Doorway was completed so he could tell them he had been inside that tunnel, and that he wasn't scared a bit.

Meanwhile Thomas was relaxing on his bed with the latest issue of *Science for Kids* magazine. It wasn't often that Thomas got to goof off while Joel was working, so Thomas was enjoying every minute of it. He had found a story about how doctors can put lights and cameras inside the human body. Using these instruments, or "scopes," they can look at the inside of organs and blood vessels without surgery.

He had finished reading and was looking back over the pictures when he heard his mother call: "Thomas, it's your night to set the table." Feeling a little hungry, he dropped his magazine, washed his hands, and headed for the delicious smells of the kitchen to get things ready.

* * * * *

Joel and Thomas loved their mother's spaghetti, so it wasn't until they had completely finished the first serving that they stopped eating long enough to talk. Their father used the opportunity to see what the boys were up to. "Did Ms. Cox give you any homework for the weekend?"

"All we have to do is figure out some things about sound waves," said Joel. He seemed proud that he was able to jump in with the answer, even though he had spent so much of the school day dreaming about the inside of that old tunnel. It was always nice to look like a good student in front of Mom and Dad.

Seconds later, there was a hissing sound coming from the kitchen. Rev. Mason got up from the table and began walking around the kitchen trying to find the source of this new noise. Mrs. Mason called out, "Honey, it looks like there's some water on the floor in front of the sink. Rev. Mason squatted down and jerked open the cabinet door. Instantly, a jet of water sprayed him right in the face, startling him. He tried to quickly pull back and stand up at the same time. The scene looked like a frog jumping backwards and upside down. "Whaaaat?" their dad shouted as he sailed backward and landed on his back with a thud. His face was wet and his hair was dripping, and the spray of water was creating a little pool of water around him. Thomas and Joel watched his face turn red as he scrambled to get back up and battle through the spray to turn the handles under the sink that would shut off the water supply.

Rev. Mason stood up and turned to face his family, with his face red, his clothes wet, his hair dripping even more, and an expression of anger on his face. Mrs. Mason and the boys looked at him in silence for about 10 seconds, then they all burst into laughter at the same time. Rev. Mason turned even redder, but then his angry face turned into a smile and he started laughing too. "I guess it's time to call a plumber!"

Rev. Mason made a phone call then went to get dried off while Thomas and Joel mopped up the water on the kitchen floor with some old towels. Mrs. Mason cleared the table knowing that all of the excitement had brought suppertime to an end. They could always have a snack later if anyone got hungry.

It was about an hour later when the plumber arrived. Thomas and Joel were curious about how he would fix whatever was wrong, so they got as close as they could to watch him work. Removing a long silver tube from under the sink, he held it up and said, "Here's where your problem is. This cold water supply line cracked. I've got extras in the truck and I'll have it replaced in a few minutes, but I would recommend that you replace both of the lines and the valves while I'm here. It won't cost much and those valves are getting hard to turn. The new style valves are much easier to operate."

Rev. Mason agreed and in two minutes the plumber was back from his truck with the supplies he needed. "Do you have a cut-off valve here in the house? I'll need the water cut off while I work."

Thomas and Joel looked at their dad. "We know where it is," Joel said. "Do you want us to go downstairs and turn off the water?" Rev. Mason nodded but, before they could leave the room, the plumber stopped them and handed them a wrench out of his tool box.

"Boys," the plumber said, "when you get the water cut off, tap on the pipe with this wrench. I'll hear it up here and it will let me know I can get started."

Excited to be a part of the repair work, Thomas and Joel headed down the stairs to the basement. Thomas said, "I'll turn off the water and you can tap the pipe." The boys went down to the storage room where the main water supply came into the house. It was a copper pipe coming out of the wall about three feet above the floor, then turning straight up toward the ceiling. The cut-off valve was a short handle with a yellow plastic coating. It was pointed straight up, parallel to the water pipe. Thomas grabbed the handle pulled it down to the right, so it was pointed sideways and in the "off" position.

Thomas moved aside and Joel started tapping on the pipe with the wrench the plumber had given him. He tapped a few times, then looked at Thomas. "How long should I keep going?" he asked. Thomas shrugged, so Joel started tapping again. He tapped for two straight minutes until his dad appeared. "Joel!" he said with urgency, "You can stop all that tapping, boys! The sound is going all over the house!" The copper pipes were carrying the sound into the kitchen, the bathrooms, and everywhere that the pipes ran under the floor.

The boys went back upstairs and finished up their homework assignments. The plumber had finished, too, and Rev. Mason had gone downstairs and turned the water back on. When he got back upstairs, he said to the boys, "What were you two telling me you needed to know about sound waves?"

Thomas said, "At school, we were talking about how sound waves travel through the air. Then Ms. Cox told us to find out if sound waves can travel through something besides the air."

Their dad said, "Well, I think you got one of your answers tonight." He looked at the boys waiting to see if they would figure it out.

After a long pause, Joel's face lit up. "The pipes!" he said.

"What about the pipes?" asked his dad.

"When I was tapping the pipe, the sound waves went through the pipe up to the kitchen," Joel said. "So I guess sound waves can travel through pipes."

"Yes, sound travels through metal objects, like pipes," Rev. Mason said. "Do you remember when our car was making that rattling noise? I couldn't tell where it was coming from because the sound was traveling through the metal frame of the car and we heard rattling everywhere."

The boys remembered well because they had been afraid one of the wheels was going to fall off but they couldn't tell which one it might be.

Their father suddenly smiled a big smile. "Hey, did I ever tell you two about the time my brother, your Uncle Mac, fastened an old wind-up alarm clock to the beams under Grandpa's house? He took the bells off and fixed it so that it would vibrate against the wood of that floor beam. Then he set it to go off at 6 o'clock that night. While we were eating supper, the alarm clock began vibrating against the floor beam. It sounded like a giant angry bumble bee was buzzing all over the house. Grandpa was walking from room to room, looking in all the closets and cabinets, and couldn't figure

out what was going on. Your Uncle Mac
was sitting across from me trying his
best to keep from laughing."

"Did Grandpa ever figure out what
was going on?" Joel asked.

"He figured it out when he saw Mac
chuckling," their dad said.

"What did Grandpa do?" Thomas
asked.

"Well, nothing right then," Rev.
Mason said. "But the next Saturday
morning, Grandpa went into my
brother's bedroom at 5 o'clock in the
morning wearing a scary Halloween
mask, stood over his bed, and growled
really loud. Mac opened his eyes, saw
that scary creature standing over him,
and screamed like a little girl. When he
calmed down, your Grandpa said, 'Now
are there any other tricks you want to
play?'"

The boys laughed at their dad's story,

but they also made mental notes about how sound waves traveled through metal pipes and wooden beams.

It was bedtime. With the combination of a busy day, the night's homework, and the excitement of the broken pipe in the kitchen, Joel and Thomas were tired and ready for sleep. But Thomas took a little longer than normal to fall asleep because he was already worrying about how things would go on tomorrow's big adventure. Would they get inside the train tunnel? What was in there? And what crazy plans did Joel have for them that could get them in big trouble?

With images of a dark, spider-filled tunnel in his mind, he finally fell asleep.

CHAPTER 4: EYE WITNESS

Joel and Thomas awakened to a perfect Saturday morning—the best of what the month of May had to offer. A cool breeze was gently stirring the leaves on the trees, the sweet smell of nearby honeysuckle and the buzz of honey bees filled the air, and everything out in the open felt the warming rays of the sun. Mornings like these were a reminder that summer was fast approaching.

"Mom, can we get breakfast at Shifflett's Market?" Mrs. Mason was enjoying the sunny morning, sitting out on their deck, reading the morning paper. From their deck you could see Buck's Elbow mountain which was now deep green with the new leaves of spring.

"I guess so," she replied. "Just stay off of the highway and be careful." Shifflett's Market was about one half mile from their house, on the main highway. But Joel and Thomas would be riding on the dirt path that ran along the edge of the field beside the highway. The road wouldn't be very busy on a Saturday morning, but it was still no place for two young boys on bicycles. "What else do you plan to do today?" their mother asked.

Thomas stood by silently, wondering how Joel would explain his plans for the day. "We're just going to ride around and stuff. You know we have that school project about the Greenwood tunnel. We'll probably ride by the Carter's farm and see what Mr. Carter remembers about the tunnel."

"That's a good idea," said Mrs. Mason. "He actually grew up in Greenwood, so he should remember a lot." She did think it was odd that Joel would be so interested in school work that he would spend a beautiful Saturday morning doing research. She thought that Thomas must have come up with the idea. "Well, be careful and don't be late coming home," she said, looking at Thomas. She knew he would keep an eye on his watch.

"Let's go, Shadow!" Joel said as they left the house. And the twins took off on their bikes for Shifflett's Market. Joel had grabbed his camouflage backpack full of equipment.

At the market, both of the boys got two warm sausage biscuits and a bottle of orange juice. They each picked out a snack for later. Joel got his favorite—a can of "beanie weenies"—and Thomas picked up two packs of peanut butter crackers. They put their selections on the counter.

"Stubby" was at the cash register. They didn't really know Stubby, but he was almost always there behind the counter, and they had heard lots of other people call him by that name. They had no idea how he got the name. "Do you boys want to charge that to your dad's account?"

Joel and Thomas nodded. They thought it was wonderful that they could get stuff at the store without money or anything. They didn't even have to tell Stubby who they were. Somehow he had known who they were the very first time they came in the store. This was one of the neat things about living in a small community.

Stubby thumbed through a file box and found a card with "Preacher Mason" written at the top in dark letters. He slid the card into the cash register, hit a button, then put the card on the counter.

"I'll get it," said Thomas before Joel could move. He picked up the ink pen on the counter and signed his name next to the amount printed on the card. At the end of the month, his mom or dad would stop by to pay off their account. Thomas felt grown up, being able to charge things at the market. They didn't have a store like this where they used to live—a store where people already knew you and you could get breakfast and stuff just by signing your name.

Sitting on a short wall outside of the market, the boys made their biscuits disappear in a hurry. "Are we really going over to Mr. Carter's farm?" Thomas asked. When Joel had mentioned it to Mom, it had caught him by surprise.

"Of course," Joel said, a little perturbed. "I wouldn't have told Mom we *were* going if we *weren't*. Besides, if we take the dirt road into the back of the Carters' farm, it will be a short cut to Greenwood!" Joel was particularly proud of that idea. He remembered old Mr. Carter saying that he drove his pickup truck down the dirt road on his way to church because it was a lot shorter that way. His wife always came the long way, but she drove their nice car. Mr. Carter liked to be the first one at church every Sunday, and Mrs. Carter preferred to take her time getting ready and read the Sunday newspaper before she left home—especially the comics.

As they drained the last drops of orange juice out of their bottles, Joel handed his can of beanie weenies to Thomas. "Let's go," Joel said. "You carry the snacks."

Thomas put the beanie weenies and crackers in the zippered pouch hanging from his bike's handle bars, next to the two juice drinks he had brought from home. Both boys threw their trash into the big can by the store's gas pumps, and took off back down the dirt path toward the road they lived on. They rode past their house, turned onto Big Creek Road, and rode about two miles to the dirt road leading into the Carter's farm. Because of a recent rain shower, the road wasn't very dusty, but there were plenty of rocks and pot holes to watch out for.

* * * * *

"The Greenwood Tunnel?" asked Mr. Carter, as he walked with the boys back to his big front porch. "What do you want to know about it?"

"Oh, anything you can tell us," Thomas said. "We're doing a school project about the tunnels that Claudius Crozet worked on back in the 1850s."

"Well, I wasn't around when the tunnels were dug, if that's what you mean," said Mr. Carter with a smile. "I may be old, but I'm not over 150 years old!"

"Oh, we didn't mean you were *that* old," said Thomas quickly. Mr. Carter looked at Thomas with his eyebrows raised. Thomas wasn't sure if his reply had made things better or worse.

"OK, boys, have a seat and I'll tell you what I know." Mr. Carter, Thomas, and Joel each found one of the white wicker chairs on the front porch to sit in. The chairs creaked a little when the three sat down. Mr. Carter had closed in his porch a couple of years back, and had put big windows all the way around. This time of year, with the sun coming in those windows, the porch was warm.

Settling down in those chairs, feeling the warm sun shining down, Thomas felt like staying a long time. But Joel's eyes were fixed on the view of the nearby mountainside where he knew the entrance to the Greenwood Tunnel lay waiting. And Thomas could tell by the look in Joel's eyes that they wouldn't be sitting on this warm porch for long.

Mr. Carter began telling the two boys about watching the trains disappearing into the tunnel and popping out of the tunnel back when he was a boy himself. He had always heard that the ground surrounding the tunnel was made up of clay and crumbling slate, which made the tunnel weaker than if it had been through solid rock. And he told Thomas and Joel that, because of the improvements in the power and speed of trains, the tunnel was considered unsafe and the entrance was closed up around 50 years ago.

"When they closed it up, did they leave

the tracks inside?" Joel asked, still dreaming about his go-cart that would race down those old abandoned rails.

"Well now, I can't say for sure," Mr. Carter said, "I was away in the Navy when the tunnel was closed up. But my guess is that they took out anything they could use elsewhere. And those steel train tracks would have been an expensive thing to leave behind."

Joel got a disappointed look on his face. Even though there was no way he was ever going to have a go-cart inside that train tunnel, just thinking it was possible was part of the excitement. "Oh, well," he thought to himself, "there still might be some kind of treasure in there, or maybe some secret passages!" And with those thoughts, his face brightened back up.

Soon the boys were back on their bikes, riding down Mr. Carter's gravel driveway toward Greenwood. Mr. Carter noticed that they were leaving in the opposite direction from which they came, but he figured two young, energetic boys like the Mason twins had big plans for a beautiful Saturday morning like this.

CHAPTER 5: OPERATION DOORWAY

As they pedaled down the driveway, Thomas felt the butterflies in his stomach. He knew the next step in today's mission called for them to cross the wild man's farm again. "How long will he keep us locked up in his barn, if he catches us?" he wondered. But all of his worrying was for nothing today, because when they got to the edge of the wild man's farm, the old pickup truck was gone.

"Shadow, this is Vanguard," Joel whispered as they crouched at the top of the hill. "Enemy fort is abandoned. The coast is clear. Move out!" Leaving their bikes in the woods, Thomas grabbed the pouch off of his handlebars containing their snacks. They scurried down the hill, through the fences, and across the open field, Joel imagined the wild man flying up the dirt driveway, dust in the air, the man's long, gray beard flapping out the window as he spotted the twin trespassers in his field. The image in his mind made his feet move even faster as they cleared the last fence and headed on toward the Greenwood Tunnel.

Having located the tunnel on their last trip, this time they headed straight for the overgrown brush which partially hid the bricks and cement of the closed-up entrance. Again, Joel noticed the small opening high on the wall to the side of the main arch. And again, the small leaves of the vines around the opening were moving in a way that indicated air was blowing out of that vent. It was too small for them to crawl through, though Joel would have given it a try if he thought there was any chance he could make it through. It would have to be much, much bigger before Thomas would think about crawling through.

But Joel already had a plan and it didn't involve crawling. "Shadow, hand me the flashlight and the rubber bands out of my backpack."

Wondering just what Joel had in mind, Thomas opened his brother's backpack. Inside were the boys' two walkie talkies that they had gotten for Christmas a couple of years earlier. Joel had also packed rubber bands, the reel from a fishing rod, a roll of tape, some rope, a flashlight, Joel's plastic binoculars, a small pad of paper, and a pencil. Thomas tried to imagine what in the world Joel was going to do with this collection of stuff.

Thomas scooped up the flashlight and rubber bands. He turned around to find Joel pulling a long straight branch out of a nearby tangle of weeds. Joel immediately went to work on the branch with his pocketknife, cutting off twigs and smoothing it down a little. Thomas wondered if he was making a walking stick. "OK," Joel said, closing up his knife and putting it back in his pocket. "Hand me the flashlight."

Thomas watched as Joel placed the flashlight against the small end of the branch, pointing outward. "I'll hold it here," Joel said. "You put the rubber bands around the flashlight and stick so it won't fall off."

When they were done, they had created a flashlight with a six-foot-long handle. "Now," Joel said, turning on the flashlight beam, "let's take a look inside this tunnel!" The boys took turns sliding the "light pole" into the air vent, sticking their heads as far into the vent as they could, and peering into the darkness. With the musty air blowing gently on their faces, they stared and squinted into the hole. As Joel took over the "light pole" again, and peered into the vent, Thomas said, "Do you smell some kind of fumes?"

Thomas said, "It's probably just something from the trains that used to go through here."

"No way!" Joel said, "Mr. Carter said that the tunnel was closed up about 50 years ago. There's no smell that lasts that long."

"Well, maybe it's coming from wherever all this air is coming from," Joel suggested.

"That's another thing," Joel said. "Where *is* all this air coming from? If the tunnel is closed up, why is there *any* air coming out?" It was a question that neither boy had an answer for.

They continued to stare. Joel even tried staring into the hole with his binoculars. But all they could see was a small patch of bricks up ahead where the end of the air vent met the curved upper wall of the tunnel.

Joel turned off the flashlight, started pulling off the rubber bands, and said to his brother, "Shadow, get the field communication gear."

Thomas looked at him for a moment. "The what?" he asked.

"The walkie talkies! Get the walkie talkies!" said Joel, frustrated that Thomas hadn't understood his new, improved name for the radios he had packed. "And I need the fishing reel, too."

As Thomas dug around in the backpack for the walkie talkies and the fishing reel, Joel went back to work on the long stick with his pocketknife, carving a notch into its smaller end where the flashlight had been. "What's this for?" Thomas asked.

"Well," said Joel, "if we can't see anything in there, maybe we can hear something in there."

Thinking that this was a big waste of time, Thomas said, "There's nothing in there to hear, and I'm getting hungry."

"Maybe, but I'll know for sure in a minute," Joel said as he tied the fishing line around the walkie talkie. Then he pushed down the "talk" button, and held it down with a rubber band. "Now, I'll lower it down into the tunnel, and you listen on the other walkie talkie."

Joel slipped the fishing line into the notch he had created on the end of the branch, and carefully guided the dangling walkie talkie into the air vent.

61

When it reached the other end of the vent, he slowly let the fishing line slip through his fingers and lowered the walkie talkie down into the old train tunnel. "Do you hear anything, Shadow?" he whispered to his brother.

"No, Vanguard. No audio information received, and we're at full volume," Thomas responded. He hoped that if he played along, maybe they could finish sooner and eat lunch. He was starving.

Joel lowered the radio a little further, and tried rotating the stick, hoping it would somehow help them hear something. "Anything now?" Joel asked.

"Negative, Vanguard." Thomas replied.

Finally Joel gave up and began pulling the walkie talkie back up. About halfway up, he hit a snag. Jiggling, tugging, letting out string and pulling it back in, Joel tried everything to get the radio back up to the end of the air vent, but nothing was working. Finally, he tugged on the string hard and felt it break. A split second later, the other walkie talkie erupted with a series of pops as the first walkie talkie hit the bottom of the tunnel.

Thomas jerked the radio away from his ear, startled by the sudden, loud noise. "What was that?" he asked. When he saw Joel pull the long stick out of the air vent with the string dangling from the end, he knew that Joel had lost the other radio. Immediately, he looked at the back of the radio in his hand. On the back, in magic marker, was written "Joel." Joel had just lost Thomas' walkie talkie in the train tunnel. "That figures," Thomas thought.

Since they hadn't been able to see anything with the flashlight or hear anything with the walkie talkie, Thomas and Joel stopped to eat the lunch snacks they had bought at Shifflett's Market that morning. Between the spoonfuls of beenie weenies, Joel continued to hold the other walkie talkie close to his ear, hoping he would hear something that would justify having lost Thomas' walkie talkie in the tunnel. And, a couple of times, he thought he heard some kind of repeating noise, like a machine running somewhere deep inside the tunnel. But it was so faint that he just wasn't sure.

Meanwhile, Thomas ate his peanut butter crackers in silence, still upset that it was *his* walkie talkie that Joel had dropped into the train tunnel, lost forever. And even if Joel offered to give him the one that was left—what good was one walkie talkie without the other?

After they had finished off their snacks, Joel got up and said, "OK, Thomas, I guess it's time to head back." He was so discouraged that their "mission" had failed that he didn't even use their code names, "Vanguard" and "Shadow." They packed up their gear, minus one walkie talkie, and headed back toward the wooded hilltop on the other side of the wild man's farm where they left their bikes.

When they got to the fence at the edge of the wild man's farm, the old battered pickup truck was still gone, letting them know that the wild man had not yet returned home. So they were able to take their time crossing the field to the other side of the farm.

Just as the boys slowly climbed through the last fence on the other side of the farm, Thomas happened to see a cloud of dust on the other side of the wild man's house. And it was being formed by the old pickup truck zooming down the driveway toward them. "Run!" yelled Thomas. And the two boys scrambled up the hill like lightening, and crouched behind some tall brush. Breathing hard from their fast climb and out of fear, they watched as the wild man stopped his truck by the old white farmhouse and climbed out. With a bag in his arms, he stared up toward the edge of the woods where the boys were now hiding. For what seemed like forever, he stood and stared in their direction, and then he turned and went into the house.

Wondering if he might come back out to chase after them, the two boys wasted no time grabbing their bikes and tearing off toward home. They were half way home when the grip of terror finally subsided, and their racing heartbeats returned to normal. The disappointments they experienced back at the tunnel were now unimportant. Thomas and Joel felt lucky to have escaped unimaginable dangers. Just a few seconds later and they would have been right in the middle of the field when the wild man returned, not knowing which way to run.

CHAPTER 6: CAVES AND COOKIES

As Mrs. Mason passed the bowl of mashed potatoes to Thomas, she asked the two boys, "So, did Mr. Carter tell you anything to help you on your train tunnel project?" Joel and Thomas nodded, their mouths full of food. The day's adventures and life-threatening dangers had given the boys quite an appetite by supper time.

Thomas chased his peas with a swig of milk, "Mr. Carter told us about seeing the trains use the tunnel when he was a kid. We can make an interview out of that for our project. That should help our grade. Teachers love interviews."

Joel liked learning and discovering, but to him grades were more of a bother than anything else. "He said the same thing you said, Dad," Joel chimed in. "The faster and bigger trains were more than the old tunnel could handle, so that's why they quit using it. But I wonder why they didn't just leave it open for people to go into?"

Rev. Mason tried to answer the question. "It was probably because of safety and money issues. The railroad company, I'm sure, didn't want to spend money keeping the tunnel safe if they didn't use it anymore. And if they weren't going to take care of it, they were probably afraid there might be cave-ins or other ways that people could get hurt inside."

"Well, it would be a lot cooler if it was

open," Joel said disappointedly.

"Actually it would be warmer if it was open," Rev. Mason said with a grin. He knew that Joel didn't mean "cool" as in "temperature," but the opportunity to teach was just too good to pass up. "You see, in a cave or tunnel like that, the temperature is influenced by the ground temperature. Deep into a hillside like that, the temperature stays around 55 degrees or so all year long. That's cooler than outside in the summer and warmer than outside in the winter. So if the tunnel was open, with a summer breeze blowing through, that would make it warmer instead of cooler. But since it's closed up, it's probably about the same temperature in there all year long. You could even use it for your home if you didn't mind your house being 10 feet wide and a mile long," he said with a smile. "It could be a long walk to the bathroom!"

Joel didn't say anything, but the idea of turning the old tunnel into a home created all kinds of pictures in his mind. And if it was really long, you might even need that go-cart just to go from room to room! That would be awesome!

Thomas had been listening and thinking, too. "But, Dad, isn't 55 degrees too cold for a house?"

"Well," his father replied, "it is a little chilly. But you wouldn't need a lot of heat to make a 55-degree room comfortable. If you think about our house, in the winter we're trying to warm it up to 65 degrees when the outside temperature is in the 30s. And in the summer we're trying to cool it down to 78 degrees when the outside temperature is in the 90s. In a cave or tunnel, you could probably just pump in outside air to warm it up in the summer, and use a heater to warm it up in the winter. Some people have actually built their homes inside of caves, and they say that it's very easy to keep it comfortable all year-round."

The conversation turned toward other matters. Mrs. Mason mentioned a phone call she had gotten that day about a church member who was released from the hospital. Mr. Mason went over the weather forecast for the week. Mrs. Mason asked her husband if he had heard the news report about criminal activity in their area. Police suspected that this was part of a much larger crime ring at work in several states. The criminals were involved in illegal drugs, counterfeit money, and other crimes.

Listening in, especially to the weather report, the boys finished off the food on their plates. But they didn't stuff themselves because Thomas and Joel had smelled the unmistakable aroma of homemade chocolate chip cookies when they had gotten back home that afternoon. And they were both praying that these cookies were not for some church meeting.

Later that night the boys found out that their prayers had been answered. While Thomas typed up information from their interview with Mr. Carter, Joel was busy making the overdue headlines for their project poster: "The Greenwood Tunnel, by Joel and Thomas Mason, Teacher: Ms. Cox, Room 14." Just for fun, he drew all the letters to look like train tracks. Those were the kind of details that his teacher, Ms. Cox, seemed to really like.

The boys were seconds from being done when Mrs. Mason came in with a tray containing two big glasses of milk and a plate of chocolate chip cookies that were begging to be eaten. Thomas counted out the cookies quickly. "Wow, four cookies apiece!" he said. Because Joel usually ate faster than Thomas, Thomas wanted to make it clear that if Joel finished his four cookies first, that was just tough. It was Thomas' nice way of saying, "Keep your fingers off of my cookies!" Mrs. Mason smiled as she headed back into the kitchen with the empty tray. She knew exactly why Thomas had made his comment. Joel knew, too. And, in a way, he was glad to know how many cookies he should eat. He wouldn't have intentionally eaten his brother's share, but he knew that after diving into homemade chocolate chip cookies, the cookies would be long gone before he would think about how many he should or should not eat.

* * * * *

That night, as they prepared for bed,

Thomas thought about their close call with the wild man on their way home that afternoon. And he wondered again what might happen to them if the wild man ever caught them on his property.

In the next room, Joel was lying in bed with the one remaining walkie-talkie pressed tight to his hear, wondering if he might hear some noise from within the tunnel, even though he knew that the other walkie-talkie was too far away and that the batteries had probably died by now, too. Still, he wondered about the sounds he thought he heard when they were still outside the tunnel—almost like a car engine. Was it his imagination? Or was it a noise from behind that wall of concrete that sealed off the tunnel from the outside world? He knew it was impossible, but it sounded like there was already a train tunnel go-cart in there! He didn't know how he would get inside that tunnel, but Joel made up his mind, as he fell asleep, that somehow he would find out whether or not there was anything important in that abandoned tunnel through the mountain.

CHAPTER 7: TACTICAL DIVERSION

As Monday morning dawned, Thomas and Joel awoke to the singing of birds and the sound of pancake batter being mixed in the kitchen. The boys quickly got dressed for school and gathered up their books and homework and loaded their backpacks. Heading for the kitchen, they knew what they were going to hear before they got there.

"Who wants pickleberry pancakes?" called Mrs. Mason as the boys stepped into the kitchen. One of the boys' favorite books from their kindergarten years mentioned "pickleberries." So, for fun, Mrs. Mason began putting green food coloring in the pancake batter and calling it "pickleberry pancakes." At first, the boys were amazed that their mother had found pickleberries to put in their pancakes. But they had figured out years ago that pickleberries were just a joke and the green coloring in the pancakes was food coloring. But Mrs. Mason still called them pickleberry pancakes, and she still put the food coloring in every batch. It was a "mom thing."

Later, with a stomach full of buttery green pancakes and syrup, washed down with orange juice, Joel and Thomas climbed aboard the bus. Kevin Freeman was already on the bus, as always. Joel spoke to him as he walked by, "Hey, Kevin." Joel and Thomas took a seat right behind him. Kevin seemed like a lonely kid. He was so much bigger than the other kids his age, and so shy, that most of the kids weren't sure what to do with him. For the first time, Kevin turned around and spoke back. "I saw you guys ride past my house Saturday morning. Where were you going?"

Joel was more than happy to share the excitement of "Operation Doorway," even if it hadn't turned out like he planned. "We went to see if we could get inside the Greenwood Tunnel. We found the entrance but it was closed up with a cement wall. We tried to look inside through a hole but we couldn't see much." Then Joel made a bold statement: "I think there's something going on inside that old tunnel."

That was the first time Thomas had heard Joel make that claim. He just sat there in shock. "Where did he get that from?" he thought. "The only thing going on in there is that *my* walkie-talkie is growing mold on the cold, damp floor of that tunnel because *he* dropped it." Thomas grew irritated all over again, but neither Kevin nor Joel seemed to notice.

"Going on? Like what?" asked Kevin.

"I don't know. Some kind of machine is running inside there. I heard it."

Thomas couldn't believe it. "I didn't hear anything," he protested.

"I know," Joel said, "but maybe it's because I was moving the walkie talkie around too much on the end of that string. Or maybe it was too close to the air vent. Anyway, after I dropped it inside, I'm sure I heard something. I just don't know what."

"Cool!" Kevin exclaimed. "Are you going to go back to the tunnel again? 'Cause if you do, I want to go, too."

Thomas could see what was coming. From what Joel had said, he knew that there was another trip to the Greenwood

Tunnel in their future. He considered the whole idea a waste of time, which wouldn't have been so bad except for the dangers of having to cross the wild man's farm again. One day, he knew, their luck would have to run out. It almost did last time.

The time left on the bus was spent with Joel giving Kevin Freeman a full account of their adventure Saturday morning. With every twist and turn of the story, Kevin was more excited about going with them next time.

Even though he dreaded another trip back to the tunnel, Thomas was glad for the chance to create a friendship with Kevin. He was especially glad now that the bus had arrived at the school and he saw two familiar female faces searching the bus windows for the Mason twins.

"Kevin," Thomas said with urgency, "can you do us a favor?"

"Like what?" Kevin asked.

"We need to get by *them*," Thomas said, with Joel's head nodding in agreement.

Kevin smiled. He may have been quiet up to now, but he was well aware of the way Sherry West and Janice Taylor had been chasing after the Mason twins all year long. "What do you want me to do?" he asked.

Together, with little time to think, the three boys cooked up a plan. Joel and Thomas were wearing matching blue jackets, and Joel had a University of Virginia Cavaliers cap in his backpack. Hoping that the girls wouldn't be able to tell which twin it was through the glare of the bus windows, Joel put on his ball cap, and waved at the girls through the window while Thomas ducked down in the seat. Then, as students began filing off the bus, the three boys all hid while Kevin put on Joel's hat and blue jacket.

It was a tight fit, but it was the only plan they had. Thomas took off his jacket and quickly stuffed it into his backpack.

The twins crouched down behind Kevin as he made his way off of the bus wearing Joel's jacket and cap. Then Kevin hopped off the bus, and pretended to straighten the cap by grabbing the visor. It was just a sneaky way of partially covering his face. First, he hid behind the crowd of students filing off of the bus, and then he began weaving through the mass of students toward the school entrance, darting back and forth to make himself hard to catch.

Sherry and Janice took off after the "mystery twin" not knowing which of their heart throbs they were chasing. They caught him just before he reached the school entrance, and jumped in front of him before he could get in the door. The big smiles on their faces quickly dissolved into complete confusion as they saw Kevin's face under that cap. It was so funny that he burst out laughing.

Thomas and Joel had already made it into the school and watched from around a corner. It was the first time they had ever heard Kevin Freeman laugh out loud, and they couldn't help but laugh themselves. But their laughter stopped suddenly when Janice and Sherry recognized their voices and turned to come after them. Now it was more than love that motivated them. Sherry and Janice had been tricked, and they had been a little embarrassed about mistaking Kevin as a "boyfriend." They had a score to settle with Thomas and Joel.

Seeing the serious, determined scowl on the girls' faces, Joel and Thomas realized that they were in an even bigger mess now. They took off for Ms. Cox's room, hoping to find protection there until Janice and Sherry had time to cool off. They dropped their backpacks in their seats, and hid in the far corner of the room with their backs to the door, pretending to look at something on a bulletin board.

Seconds later, the two girls arrived at Ms. Cox's open doorway. Seeing the two girls, and the perturbed expressions on their faces, Ms. Cox wandered over to the two brothers and said, "Thomas and Joel, what have you two done? There are two very upset girls looking for you out there."

As Thomas and Joel explained what they had done with Kevin Freeman's help, Ms. Cox realized that the girls weren't just fooled by the boys' plan, but were also embarrassed. And Ms. Cox also knew that she would need to step in to help fix this little mess. So she told the twins that she wanted to talk to them later in the day about better ways to handle the girls. Then Ms. Cox went out into the hallway and let the girls know that she knew about the trick the boys had played on them, and she would be talking to them later in the day. Ms. Cox also asked the girls to wait until lunch to go looking for Thomas and Joel. "Girls, you have to understand," Ms. Cox said, taking them under her wing, "boys just aren't as good at relationships as attractive young ladies like yourselves. And when they see two pretty girls waiting for them before school even starts, they just don't know how to act. You should see how hard it is for them to concentrate in my class knowing what lovely young ladies are interested in them. So you would really be helping me as a teacher if you could wait, at least until lunchtime, to talk with them."

Ms. Cox's "counseling" seemed to make the girls feel better, and made them more tolerant of the boys' sneaky get-away scheme. But the Mason twins weren't sure whether to feel better or not. They had no idea what Ms. Cox would say when they talked with her later. And, while they weren't interested in "love," it really wasn't their intention to upset Sherry and Janice. And Joel began to wonder about one other problem: "How am I going to get my jacket back before recess?"

CHAPTER 8: GAMMA TEAM IS FORMED

Lunchtime finally arrived and Ms. Cox lined the students up to head to the cafeteria. She asked her students to follow another teacher who was headed that way, and she kept Thomas and Joel behind to talk to them about Janice and Sherry.

"Boys," she said gently but firmly, "I know you're not comfortable with the attention Janice and Sherry show you, but I still want you to be polite to them. Nobody likes to be embarrassed, *especially* a fifth grade girl." She asked them to make a point of apologizing to the girls for tricking them that morning.

They left to catch up to their classmates who had just gotten seated in the cafeteria. Joel and Thomas found seats at the table where their new friend from the bus, Kevin Freeman, was sitting. Joel was very relieved to see that Kevin had Joel's jacket and hat with him. As they ate lunch, Kevin wanted to talk to them about their plans for finding a way into the old train tunnel. He wanted to make sure he got in on the adventure.

"How are you guys going to get inside the tunnel?" Kevin asked.

"Maybe there's a secret entrance they left when they closed it up," Joel said. "Besides, I'm sure I heard some kind of noise coming from in there. Maybe someone already found a way in."

"What kind of noise?" Kevin asked.

"Like a machine running. And there

was air blowing out of a vent hole in the cement wall. How can air come out if there isn't some place for it to blow in?" Joel said.

Thomas had to admit that the blowing air had made him curious, but his curiosity wasn't strong enough to overcome his worry about what might go wrong. What if they found a way in, but couldn't find their way back out? What if the tunnel was full of bats, or an angry bear? What if messing around in there caused it to cave in? Thomas remembered seeing a TV show about some people who were trapped in a mine shaft when it caved in. It could happen!

Kevin interrupted Thomas' thoughts, "Hey, guys, I have an idea! I live a lot closer to the tunnel, so why don't you guys sleep over at my house on Friday night and we can go explore the tunnel together on Saturday morning? Our class is doing the same project, so I can tell my Mom that we're going to take pictures to use for school."

Joel loved the idea, and Thomas thought it might be nice to have someone to hang out with besides just his brother. So Kevin said he would talk to his Mom about a sleep-over and ask her to call the Masons to set it all up if it was OK.

Joel got out a pen and starting making a list on his napkin. These are the things you'll probably need for our mission," Joel said to Kevin.

Kevin looked over the list. Some of it made sense: a flashlight, rope, pocket knife. But other items made Kevin wonder what Joel had in mind. Why would they need 9-volt batteries and duct tape? Kevin looked at Thomas with a puzzled expression, but Thomas just shook his head as if to say, "Don't ask."

"I don't think I have some of these

things," Kevin said.

"That's OK," Joel said. "Just let me know what you've got and I'll see about getting the rest. Do you have a backpack you can put stuff in?"

"I've got my school backpack," Kevin said.

"It might get dirty," Thomas said. He was imagining a dark, dirty, bat-filled, spider web-covered place. After all, that train tunnel had been closed up for a long time. He wouldn't want to take *his* school backpack in there!

"Well, I've got my old backpack from First Grade, but it's a little embarrassing," Kevin said.

"What's embarrassing about it," Joel asked.

"Well, I was really into Bert and Ernie from Sesame Street back then..." Kevin didn't finish his explanation, but Joel and Thomas were giving him a "we understand" look. They were remembering the things they were obsessed with back then, most of which had already been put in bags and donated to local thrift stores. But every so often they found a Blue's Clues sticker on an old notebook or a Dora the Explorer pencil hiding in their rooms.

"It's just going to be us three," Thomas said. "So nobody else will see it."

Joel almost shouted, "Gamma Team!" He looked at Thomas and Kevin and said it again, "Gamma Team! It's perfect."

Thomas was a little surprised by the suddenness of Joel's outburst, but there wasn't much his brother said that surprised him. On the other hand, Kevin was totally confused, "What's a 'Gamma Team'?"

"We are!" Joel said, "The three of us together. That's what we can call ourselves. There are three of us and *gamma* is the third letter in the Greek alphabet."

"We need a name for ourselves?" Kevin asked.

Thomas agreed. They didn't need any more code names, but he had stopped asking questions like that a long time ago. Joel, on the other hand, couldn't imagine the three of them not having a name for themselves on this adventure.

Not getting an answer to his first question, Kevin asked, "How do you know Greek letters?"

Thomas explained, "Our dad is a pastor, and he has a lot of books on Greek because part of the Bible was written in Greek. So he talks about that stuff sometimes."

Lunchtime was almost over, and it was time for the boys to line up with their classes and head back to their rooms. Joel, Thomas, and Kevin planned to talk more about the plans for their adventure on the bus that afternoon.

* * * * *

Math and recess filled the afternoon. The boys heard the intercom speaker pop to life in their room, and the voice of the Principal followed reminding the students and teachers about upcoming events and congratulating some of the students and teachers on some special accomplishments. Soon afterward, the boys heard the final bell ringing in the hallway.

When the final bell rang, marking the end of the school day, Thomas and Joel headed for the bus. As expected, Sherry and Janice were waiting for them on the sidewalk of the bus loop, and even though the girls were waiting for them, Janice and Sherry still didn't seem happy to see them.

Thomas and Joel both stopped and spoke to them, "We're sorry we played a trick on you this morning," the boys said, not knowing what else to say. They waited while Janice and Sherry looked at each other. The girls seemed a little surprised by their apology and not sure what to say. After a few moments of awkward silence, the boys said, "See you tomorrow!" and they headed for their bus. Kevin was already sitting in his usual spot, and he waved at the twins to come sit with him.

"Hey, you guys," Kevin said, "if you get to come over, and if the weather is OK, maybe we could sleep in my treehouse fort. My dad builds houses for a living, and he built me a really nice treehouse. It's got a roof, electricity, and I can close up the window if it's cold or rainy. As long as you've got a warm sleeping bag, it's pretty comfortable."

Thomas responded, "Dad and Mom have taken us camping several times, so we both have good sleeping bags."

"Yeah," Joel said, "that would be awesome. Then Gamma Team can finish planning the mission to the tunnel in secret."

Because Joel and Thomas got on the bus after Kevin and got off the bus before him, they had never seen his house. They both really hoped that Kevin's parents would be OK with his sleepover idea, and that their parents would say it was OK with them, too.

When they got home, they eagerly waited to hear the phone ring in hopes that it would be Kevin's mom arranging their weekend visit with their new friend and fellow member of "Gamma Team."

CHAPTER 9: THE FREEMAN FORTRESS

When Kevin, Joel, and Thomas knew that their weekend sleepover was approved by both sets of parents, it made the school week drag by even slower. But eventually Friday afternoon arrived. Thomas and Joel had their sleeping bags and other items already sitting in the back of the car ready for their ride over to Kevin Freeman's house. Kevin's mom had invited them to come over immediately after school, and had checked to make sure that the boys liked pizza. They loved it, and were even more excited knowing what they would be having for supper.

Kevin's house was an old farmhouse that sat back off of the road. The house was in great shape and had a big front porch. Kevin's mother met them at the door and invited the boys and their mother in. The twins dropped their sleeping bags and backpacks on the front porch and followed their friend through the door. Mrs. Mason mentioned how beautiful the Freeman's house was, and how much she loved how it looked inside. Kevin's mom told about them buying the house when it needed a lot of work, and that Kevin's dad had done all of the renovations himself.

While Kevin's mom gave Mrs. Mason a tour of the house, Kevin invited the boys to his room which was upstairs. Kevin was an only child, so there was no big brother or little sister around and he had a large bedroom all to himself. As soon as they walked into the room, it was clear that Kevin was into airplanes. All kinds of model planes hung from the ceiling on fishing line so thin that they seemed to be flying. There were small planes like the ones Joel and Thomas had seen flying low over the mountains behind their house, and passenger jets like the ones that left a white streak high in the sky. There were fighter jets and cargo jets. Kevin had a big poster of an SR-71 Blackbird spy plane on the wall. Joel and Thomas had never seen a plane like it, but the words at the bottom of the poster identified it for them. In a corner of the room was a work table with a desk lamp and some tools and glue. There was an open box with plastic parts inside— wings, pieces of a jet engine, landing gear. It looked like Kevin was about to put together another model plane.

Joel pointed to the model planes hanging above them. "Did you make all of those?" he asked.

Kevin said, "Yeah, I have an uncle who is in the Air Force, and he gives me model planes for my birthday every year. Oh, and check this out." Kevin opened his closet door, reached into a box on the shelf, and pulled out a long knife in a leather sheath. "At Christmas, my uncle gave me this Air Force survival knife. If a pilot gets shot down in enemy territory, he has to know how to hide from the enemy and survive until they can rescue him."

Joel and Thomas were fascinated by Kevin's knife. It had a long blade that was sharp on one edge and rough like a saw on the other edge. "What's in there?" Joel asked, pointing to a small pouch on the sheath.

Kevin snapped open the pouch and

pulled out a small rectangular stone. "It's a sharpening stone for keeping the knife sharp."

"Dude, you totally need to bring that with us on our mission tomorrow," Joel said.

Kevin had never taken the knife anywhere. "I don't want it to get messed up," he said.

"You can just keep it in your backpack. You won't need to take it out unless it's mission critical," Joel said.

Kevin and Thomas looked at each other when Joel said "mission critical." Kevin was learning how much Joel loved using those kinds of phrases. Still not sure it was a good idea, Kevin grabbed his Bert and Ernie backpack, zipped it open, and dropped in the knife.

"Do you guys want to see my treehouse?" Kevin asked.

"For sure," Thomas said. So Kevin

headed out of the room and down the stairs with the twins right behind him. As they went out the door, Thomas and Joel noticed that their mom had already left.

"Grab your stuff," Kevin said as he jumped off the porch and headed around the house.

Kevin led the boys to the edge of the woods behind his house. When Joel and Thomas looked up, their eyes almost popped out of their heads. They were expecting a rough plywood box like every other treehouse they had ever seen. Instead, they saw a camouflage-painted fort with a green tin roof. It was square in shape, about 8 feet in each direction. A small pipe ran up the side of the tree carrying the electricity to the treehouse.

Thomas looked at the tree, and saw a door on the side of the treehouse and a small platform outside of the door with a railing around it. There was a ladder that appeared to be fastened to the outside of the fort next to the door. But instead of extending down to the ground, the ladder extended up above the top of the elevated fort. "How do you get up there?" he asked.

Kevin pulled a remote control out of his pocket. Thomas recognized it as a garage door opener. Kevin pressed the button and the twin boys watched as the ladder began slowly descending toward the ground as a motor hummed inside the fort. It was so awesome that even Joel was speechless.

When the ladder was about a foot off of the ground, a bracket on the top of the ladder slid into a bracket on the side of the fort, and the motor stopped. Kevin climbed up the ladder, stepped onto the platform and opened the low door, disappearing inside. After about five seconds, he stuck his head out and said, "Throw me your stuff!" Kevin said. It took the boys a couple of tries to throw the sleeping bags high enough for Kevin to catch them. When their stuff was all inside the fort, Kevin called out, "Come on up, you guys!"

Joel climbed up and followed Kevin into the treehouse. Thomas followed him, testing the ladder just to make sure it was safe even though he had just seen two other people climb up with no problems. As Joel and Thomas moved through the door, they saw the nicest tree house they had ever been in... though they had probably only been in three or four ever.

"Dad put foam in the walls to keep it warmer out here," Kevin said. Around the top of the ceiling there was a string of white LED Christmas lights, and there was a small heating fan in the corner to take the chill away on cold nights. A small bookshelf in the corner held comic books, a deck of cards, a flashlight, a package of markers, a spiral notebook, and some action figures. The floor was covered with a green carpet, like they use on a miniature golf course. The walls were a smooth white paneling with some names and dates written in scattered places. On one wall was a big Star Wars poster with the Death Star in the middle and various characters pictured around it. In one corner was a bean bag chair.

Kevin got the markers off the shelf and held them out to Thomas and Joel. "When I have new friends in the fort, I get them to write their names and date on the wall. Pick a spot."

Joel and Thomas searched for the perfect spot and added their names and the date to the others on the walls. Joel used the blue marker, and Thomas used the black one. Then Joel got the green marker and added "Operation Doorway" next to his name. *~~op/ ~ /7:~~ ~~/~~ ~~3/~~ ~~22~~*

After putting the markers away and admiring their signatures, the boys settled in and leaned back against the wall with their sleeping bags as cushions, except for Kevin who plopped down in his bean bag chair. As the air hissed out of the seams, Kevin looked over at the twins and asked, "So what's the plan?"

That was all Joel had been thinking about. "A way in. We've already seen the outside of the tunnel. We've got to find a way inside. Maybe the railroad people left a way for them to inspect the tunnel so that there wouldn't be a big cave in. Or maybe somebody else dug a hole that leads into the tunnel. Mr. Carter said it had been closed up for 50 years. That's plenty of time for somebody to figure out how to get in there. Besides, like I told you, I heard something in there. If something is going on in there, then there has to be a way in."

"Well," Kevin thought out loud, "if people are going in and out of there, especially if they are doing something in there, there will probably be a path or road to where they are going in, right?"

Before Thomas or Joel could respond, a two-note sound played from a box on the wall, *bing-bong.* "What was that?" Thomas asked.

"That's the signal from my mom that it's supper time. My dad put in a doorbell so they could let me know when it was time to come in for supper or bedtime or whatever."

"So cool," Joel said in a whisper.

The boys climbed back down the ladder and turned toward the house, but Joel stopped. "Hey, is our stuff going to be safe while we're gone?"

Kevin smiled, pushed the button on his remote control, and the ladder slowly rose into the air, preventing anyone from entering his elevated fortress.

CHAPTER 10: ZERO HOUR

It was exactly 9:00 in the morning— "Oh Nine Hundred," Joel said as he looked at his watch—when the boys left the Freeman house for their mission to find a way into the old train tunnel. Kevin's mom had fueled them up with a delicious pancake breakfast. Kevin told her that they were going to go check out the old tunnel that they had been learning about in school, but he didn't mention that they were determined to find a way inside.

This time they were on foot, since Joel

and Thomas hadn't brought their bikes, but they didn't have very far to go. It only took them 10 minutes to arrive at the edge of the wild man's farm. Thomas could feel the knots forming in his stomach as they got closer. Now that all three of them had to cross the property, it was going to be even harder to escape the old man's notice.

At the top of the hill, Joel held up his hand and whispered loudly, "Hold up, Gamma Team!" He opened his backpack and got out the cheap binoculars.

"What are you looking for?" Kevin asked.

Thomas spoke quietly, "We are looking for the scary old man who lives here. Last time he nearly caught us."

"What happens if he catches us?" Kevin asked.

"We don't know," Thomas said, "but he looks kind of crazy. We saw him up close at the hardware store one day. It reminded me of a guy I saw in a scary movie who tried to chop people up with an ax."

Kevin wasn't convinced there was a problem, but this was no time to question his friends.

"Coast is clear, Gamma Team," Joel said. "We go on three. One, two, *THREE!*"

The boys took off across the field, running by a cow who seemed a little concerned at the intruders in its field. Holding their backpacks tight, they jumped over a few cow piles, then threaded themselves through the barbed wire fence on the far side. What they didn't see was the tall, thin, bearded figure standing just inside the entrance of the old barn, watching them like a hawk as they ran across his property.

Safely across the farm, they caught

their breath, then headed for the tunnel entrance they had visited before. "What's the plan?" Kevin asked.

The night before, as the boys lay in their sleeping bags in the treehouse waiting for sleep to overpower their excitement, Joel had mapped it all out in his head. They would climb up the hill directly over-top of the tunnel and try to follow it as best they could. With three of them searching, they could spread out— one directly over the tunnel, one far to the left, and the other far to the right— all three looking for any sight of a hole, path, or hatch that might be a way in.

The hillside over the tunnel was rough and overgrown. Briars, brush, trees, and vines made movement a lot harder than Joel had imagined. The boys struggled to make progress, trying to avoid the thorns, and weaving around the thick growth, while trying to keep moving as straight as possible. After an hour, they were tired, thirsty, and disappointed. This was not the exciting adventure any of them had imagined. They met in the middle and opened up the water bottles that Kevin's mom had given them. While no one said it, they were all wondering whether it was time to admit defeat and go back to the treehouse for the day. But before any of them could say a word, they heard a large engine start up, get louder, and then the sound of gears shifting. The sound was coming from just over the next hill.

"That sounds like a truck," Kevin said.

"What's a truck doing in the middle of the woods?" Joel said, not so much asking a question but pointing out the strangeness of it and wondering what it might mean.

"Maybe we're on someone's private property," Thomas said, with worry in his voice.

Kevin was standing up, "OK, let's go find out."

"Gamma Team on the move!" Joel said with renewed excitement.

The boys picked up their backpacks, no longer worried about spreading out, and weaved their way through the brush. They climbed the hill, moving more slowly as they reached the top, being careful to stay hidden behind the growth. There wasn't any truck in sight, but there was a rough road... really just two bare ruts through the woods the same distance apart as the tires on a car or truck. The boys could see where small trees and bushes had been cut back and the leaves had been smashed down flat. The side-by-side paths weaved around trees and rocks and stopped by a set of green metal doors that leaned back into the hillside. They were the kind of doors that usually led down to someone's storm cellar. A big fuel tank sat on cement blocks a few feet from the doors.

The boys stared as far down the path as they could see, wondering if the truck would be back. They just stood there for a while, and then Joel said, "This is it! This is what we were looking for! That has *got* to be a way into the tunnel! What else could it be?"

Thomas and Kevin were sure he was right, but the stranger or strangers driving through the woods had them wondering how smart it was to snoop around. And they wondered when whoever had been there would be back.

Joel bounded down the hill right for the metal doors. Thomas and Kevin followed behind cautiously. There were mounds of dirt and rock that had a few weeds growing on them. "I bet these dirt piles are from where they dug down to reach the tunnel!"

The green metal doors were closed, and a metal plate and padlock secured the entrance. Kevin examined the padlock. "Guys, they didn't lock it shut. The padlock is hanging open. Why put a lock on here if you don't lock it shut?"

Thomas spoke up, "I bet they're coming back in a few minutes. We'd better get out of here."

Joel desperately wanted to see the inside of that tunnel so he gathered Gamma Team for a quick pep talk. "Look, let's just run in there, take a look, and then run back out. They'll never know we were here, and we will have accomplished our mission. We can be in and out in a minute."

Joel paused for about five seconds waiting for an objection, and when neither Thomas nor Kevin responded, he grabbed his backpack, removed the open lock from the latch, and started pulling open one of the doors. A set of wooden stairs disappeared into the darkness of the passageway. Joel dropped his backpack, looked at Thomas and Kevin, and asked, "Everybody got their flashlight? We're going to need it." He pulled his flashlight out, zipped the backpack up, and grabbed it up as he shined a beam of light down the stairs.

As the boys moved slowly down the stairs, Joel was completely caught up in the adventure. Meanwhile, Thomas worried that, if someone came along and shut those doors and locked them, they'd be trapped down there for... forever!

The dark passageway seemed long as they left the bottom of the stairs and walked forward into the darkness. The passageway sloped downward, and there were wooden posts along the walls that supported beams in the ceiling. Behind the posts and the overhead beams were sheets of plywood to keep the passageway from caving in. There were light bulbs every ten feet or so along the left wall, but none of them were lit. The boys hadn't seen a switch anywhere to turn them on, so they continued forward with only their flashlights fighting the deepening darkness.

The farther they traveled from those metal doors, the more nervous Thomas got, and the more excited Joel got. Kevin was pretty nervous, too. "We need to move faster, so we can see the tunnel, then get back out in case somebody comes back," Kevin said.

Just then the small passage ended in a large open area that stretched out to the left and right. The boys stepped out into a large brick-lined tunnel with high, arched ceilings. It was creepy and amazing all at the same time. The size of the tunnel seemed to swallow the light from their flashlights. There were three little spots of light moving through the darkness as the boys shined their lights, but everywhere else around them was darkness.

All three boys got caught up in the wonder of the tunnel. As they felt the cold bricks, saw the cobwebs, and admired the size of the space and the high ceilings of this underground world, they forgot about how much time was going by. Their voices and sounds echoed off of the hard walls, reflected back by the curved surfaces, making every noise and word seem louder.

Joel shined his light over the floor of the tunnel to see if the rails were still there. He was disappointed to see that they had been removed before the tunnel was sealed up. "Well, there goes the train tunnel go-cart idea," he thought.

Then Joel moved his flashlight up. "What's that?" Joel said, pointing his flashlight down the tunnel to the left.

All three boys pointed their lights in the same direction, and the moving beams of their flashlights illuminated a tall curtain of clear plastic. Actually, it looked like a giant room made out of clear plastic, the kind of plastic you lay down on the floor when you're painting a room to keep paint off of the floor. As they moved closer, they saw a wooden frame with the plastic stapled to it. The big rectangular room of clear plastic sat in the middle of the tunnel, with a few feet of space between the plastic and the tunnel's brick walls on each side. It was higher than a regular room, but it still didn't come close to the high ceiling of the train tunnel arching over it.

"Should we look inside?" Kevin asked cautiously. But before he could answer, a noise erupted from further down in the tunnel beyond the plastic room. It was the engine noise that Joel had heard on their last trip when he dropped the walkie talkie through the vent hole—the noise of an electrical generator. Two seconds later, the room made of plastic was filled with light, lighting up the entire area around it. The sudden brightness forced the boys to squint as their eyes adjusted to the brilliant flood of light. Now they could see the tunnel walls and ceiling, and the rough floor scattered with debris, in complete detail. But there was no time to enjoy their new view, because they also heard loud, angry voices from the side passageway—voices that were rapidly getting closer.

CHAPTER 11: HIDE AND SEEK

"Hide!" Joel said in a loud whisper, and all three boys took off for the only hiding place they could think of in the open space of the tunnel. With their backpacks bouncing on their backs, they ran along the far wall between the bricks of the tunnel and the glowing plastic room, hoping to find a place behind it to hide.

The room was surprisingly long— maybe longer than their school gym. From the light that streamed through the clear plastic, they could see where the engine sound was coming from. A big electrical generator, about half as big as a washing machine sat in the middle of the tunnel floor. Thick black wires ran from the generator toward the glowing plastic room. Beyond the generator the light faded into the darkness of the continuing tunnel.

Running past the generator into the darkness, the boys saw a pile of building materials—wood planks and studs, and boxes of nails screws and plastic sheeting. It looked like someone was planning to build another big plastic room. They dove into the shadows behind the building materials, lying flat on the tunnel's floor. The sharp edges of the rocks on the floor pushed up against their ribs uncomfortably. The boys were breathing hard, and they could taste the damp dust from the floor as it got pulled into their mouths. Lying there, trying to calm their breathing and to be at least quieter than the generator running nearby, they waited, trembling in fear.

As they carefully peered through gaps in the pile of building materials, they could see through the hazy plastic into the brightly lit room. They saw what looked like a greenhouse. It looked like rows of green plants on shelves built like stairs, one on the left side of the plastic room and one on the right. Each long shelf of plants had another one behind it that was about a foot higher, with the highest shelf about five feet off the floor. There was a walkway about four feet wide between the two shelves. Over the shelves hung bright lights in two long rows, one on each side, shining down on the plants and filling the plastic room with light.

When the boys saw two figures moving toward them between the two racks of plants, they flattened themselves even more into the rocky floor, behind the pile of wood and boxes. The wrinkled plastic distorted the images of two men moving toward them inside that room. But, in spite of the fuzzy outlines, they could tell one of the men was tall and thin, and the other—the one who was still shouting—was a little heavier and average height. The noise of the generator was so loud that they couldn't hear exactly what the men were saying, but they were still shouting loud enough to be heard over the drone of the engine noise.

The men came out of the plastic on the side next to where the boys were hiding. They peered out into the shadows, and walked over as far as the generator. The three boys held their breath in motionless silence in the damp dust of the tunnel floor. Thomas could feel and hear his heart beating so hard that he was sure others could hear it, too. The look on Kevin's face seemed to express the same thought. But Joel's mind was busy coming up with options: they could run further into the darkness. They could try to run around the men and get to the tunnel's exit. They could wait for the men to leave. That was about all he could come up with at this point.

As the men got closer, they could hear the shorter man's angry words. "Do you *want* to go to back to jail? Is that it? Was it that great last time? How stupid! That lock is the only thing keeping this operation hidden from the cops!"

The taller man said, "OK, OK, I said I was sorry!"

The two men scanned the darkness behind the generator, looking over at the pile of building supplies with a long, careful gaze.

As the boys listened, pressing themselves hard against the floor from their faces to their feet, they didn't hear any more talking from the two men. Were they still standing there? Had they walked away? Every second felt like an hour as they waited and wondered what was happening on the other side of this pile of materials. Joel tried looking behind them, hoping that, if the men were still there, they would be casting shadows on the tunnel walls behind them, and he would be able to guess at their movements. But the darkness behind them was so deep that it swallowed the light and gave no clue about what was happening ahead of them.

Suddenly, there was total silence as the generator stopped running. And, when it stopped, the bright lights inside the plastic room went dark. They were surrounded by silence and darkness. The boys could hear one another breathing as they lay motionless in the darkness, still scared to death. It seemed like forever before Kevin finally broke the silence with a whisper. "Is it safe for us to get up?" Then there was more silence as the boys waited to see if that whisper reached any ears besides their own.

When nothing happened, Joel lifted his head from the dusty floor and peered into the darkness beyond the pile of building supplies. In the pitch black darkness he could see nothing—not a speck of light, or even a faint glow. It appeared that they were totally alone. "It looks safe. Let's get out of here!" he whispered.

One by one their three flashlights clicked on, piercing the darkness. All three boys instinctively scanned the space ahead for any sign of the men who had almost caught them earlier. When they were satisfied that the men were gone, the boys made their way out from their hiding place and started walking toward the plastic room. Joel couldn't resist moving the plastic aside and peeking into this strange space. Thomas and Kevin followed him in. As they scanned the room with their flashlights, they saw stair-step shelves filled with long rows of plants. Light fixtures, now turned off, hung above them, suspended on the wooden frame. Wires ran across the ceiling and a hose connected to a large water tank ran down the walkway between the plants on each side. "Why would anyone grow plants down here in the..."

Before he could finish his sentence, a voice boomed out behind them. "Hold it right there!" They spun around to see the shorter man coming through the plastic behind them. He flipped a lever on an electrical box and the room went from dark to blindingly bright light. "You've got nowhere to run. Ain't that right, partner?"

From the other end of the long aisle between the plants, the only other exit, the taller of the two men said, "Yep, that's right!" as he walked toward the boys. They were trapped and too scared to move.

The taller man stopped four feet away from the boys with his hands out, ready to grab them if they tried to run. "So what do we do with them?" he asked his partner.

"Get their backpacks and their flashlights," the shorter man said. "And check their pockets to make sure they don't have anything else on them. We need to tie them up until we can check with the boss about what we should do with them."

The tall man grabbed Joel, who was closest to him, and grabbed his flashlight and pulled off his backpack, tossing them down the aisle behind him. Then he checked his pockets and found a pocket knife that he also tossed to the floor. One by one, he checked all three boys' pockets, and tossed their backpacks and flashlights to the side, and then ordered them—first, Joel, then Thomas, and finally, Kevin—to sit on the floor.

When all three boys were sitting, the shorter man walked over to a table that held some tools, a tool box, and several empty pots. A large trashcan sat beside it with a black plastic trash bag inside. A roll of extra trash bags lay beside it. There were two large bags labeled "Potting Soil" under the table. The man opened the toolbox and grabbed a handful of plastic cable ties, and moved toward them. Joel and Thomas recognized them as something their dad called "zip ties." They had some around the house, and they had seen their dad use them to hold various things in place.

The man with the cable ties stood them up one at a time and used the plastic ties like handcuffs to secure their wrists behind their backs. "Now, put your feet together," he ordered each boy. Then he used a cable tie around their ankles so they couldn't run. All three boys were pushed back down into a sitting position on the hard damp floor.

Finally, the two men dragged the boys by the feet to the bottom of one of the plant shelves and used more cable ties to fasten their ankles to the framework of the shelves so they couldn't hop or crawl out of place. They were lined up with Joel and Thomas on the ends and Kevin wedged in between.

With all three boys bound up, hand and foot, and fastened to the frame of the shelving units, the taller of the two men looked at his partner and said, "Now what?"

"Now we tell the boss what happened, and find out what to do. And *you're* taking the blame for this mess by the way!" the shorter man said as he squinted his eyes and poked his finger toward the taller man. Then he looked over at the boys and said ominously, "Sit tight, boys. We'll be back soon!" Then the two men walked down the long row of plants and disappeared through a slit in the plastic into the darkness of the surrounding tunnel.

When it seemed certain that the men were gone, Thomas broke the silence. Shaking with fear and with a tremble in his voice, he asked, "What are they going to do to us?"

Joel spoke next. With fear, but also with a growing determination, he said, "They aren't doing anything to us, because we're getting out of here!" With that, Joel and Thomas began pulling and twisting at their plastic restraints. The cable ties cut into their wrists as they struggled, and the shelving units didn't so much as tremble as they jerked their legs back and forth. After about five minutes of pulling and tugging, their wrists were almost bleeding, and they were out of breath, but they were still tightly bound.

Thomas looked over at Kevin. He was just sitting there staring at his feet. Thomas asked him, "What are you doing?" Joel stopped to look over at Kevin, too. He was still calmly staring at his feet, concentrating hard.

Slowly and calmly, Kevin said, "OK, I need you guys to scoot over and give me some room for this to work."

"For what to work?" Joel asked.

"You'll see," Kevin said.

Thomas and Joel wiggled around until their hips were about two feet away from Kevin. Then Kevin laid back and started twisting around. He began rocking from side to side, bending his knees, and walking his shoulders down toward his feet. His size made it awkward.

"What are you doing?" Thomas asked.

Without saying a word, Kevin continued to rock back and forth, twisting his shoulders until his fingertips just reached the back of his shoe. He hooked his fingertips into his shoes and pulled his feet toward him as hard as he could. Now he could touch ankles. He used his head and shoulders to push his hands down as far as possible. Then he began sliding his right pants leg up, just a fraction of an inch at a time. With his wrists still bound together, his fingers on each hand faced one another like the legs of some insect, slowly walking up his leg. Thomas and Joel watched, impressed at how flexible this big friend of theirs was. And what Kevin lacked in flexibility he made up for in desperate determination.

Kevin's finger tips began pulling at his sock, slowly dragging it down and bunching it up at the ankle. Then Joel and Thomas both saw it—the leather sheath of Kevin's survival knife.

"You've got your knife in your sock?" Joel asked excitedly. "I thought you put that in your backpack!"

"I did," Kevin said. "But I was still worried about it getting lost or messed up, so I put it in my sock and pulled my jeans down over it." Now Kevin had the knife, in its leather holder, completely in his hands. There was a click as Kevin unsnapped the strap around the knife handle. He worked his fingers to pull the knife out of the leather case, then rocked himself hard side to side until he was on his right side. Concentrating and feeling his way, he turned the knife so that the blade was against the plastic ties on his wrist with the handle extending down into his hands. Working his fingers to push the knife up and down as he held it against the plastic, he began slowly cutting through the plastic, trying his best not to cut himself on the sharp blade. As he cut, he also pulled hard against the ties. It seemed like nothing was happening until, suddenly, the plastic popped in half and his wrists flew apart.

Kevin rolled onto his back, sat up and used the knife to cut the plastic ties on his ankles. Then he reached over and did the same for Thomas and Joel, sliding the knife under the plastic, blade up, and sawing upward so that he wouldn't cut his friends as he freed them. Then, with even more care, he cut their hands free.

Rubbing his red, aching wrists, Joel said, "Kevin, you are a genius. Now let's get out of here!"

CHAPTER 12: THE GREAT ESCAPE

The boys grabbed their backpacks and flashlights, and ran toward the end of the plant-filled room. They paused for a second as they ran out into the darkness, giving their eyes a moment to adjust. The glow of the room behind them helped them see a short distance ahead. Even better, they noticed the row of lights along the wall that they had seen when they stepped down into the tunnel entrance. The lights had been off then, but now they glowed brightly, lighting the way to the passageway that led to the outside.

Running as fast as they could, they headed down the tunnel, turned right into the passageway, and ran for the steps. Running up the steps, Joel pushed on the steel doors, but they wouldn't open. Coming up beside him, Kevin gave it his hardest push, but it was just as immovable. All three boys pushed in unison, and still the doors didn't move. "They locked the doors," Thomas said. "They locked us in down here. What do we do now?"

Kevin, feeling a new boldness after having recued them from the bondage of the cable ties, suggested a plan. "Let's go back into the tunnel and find a place to hide in the opposite direction from the plant room. When they come back, as soon as they go into the plant room, we can run out of here!"

With a nod, Joel said, "Good plan!

Let's go!" The boys ran to the tunnel end of the entrance passage. Shining their flashlights to the right, into the part of the tunnel they hadn't explored, they scanned for a place to hide. They knew they needed to be close enough to the exit passageway to get to it quickly, but still far enough away that they wouldn't be noticed.

"There's no place to hide," Joel said with worry in his voice. "It's just wide open space. What do we do?"

Kevin wanted badly to come up a solution that would make his plan work, but he couldn't think of a good solution. All three boys knew that crouching in the dark just hoping they wouldn't be seen wasn't a good plan in this dangerous situation. The three boys stood there for a few seconds in silence, still moving their flashlights back and forth, hoping to discover a solution.

"Joel, give me your flashlight," Thomas said with urgency.

"What? Why?" Joel asked.

"Just trust me. I think this will work," Thomas said. Grabbing Joel's flashlight from his loose grip, Thomas ran as fast as he could toward the glowing plastic of the plant room. Running down the long aisle toward the place where the boys had been tied up, Thomas pulled three of the large black plastic trash bags off of the roll by the work table. Holding them tightly, he stepped out of the back of the plant room. Walking a couple of steps, he laid down his flashlight with the beam shining on the plastic. Then, running toward the pile of building supplies, he carefully positioned Joel's flashlight so that its light could be seen by anyone standing outside the back of the plant room.

Running back to the plant room,

Thomas ran down the long aisle, out of the far end through the plastic, and into the darkness. Slowing down and breathing hard, Thomas looked hard into the dark for the rest of Gamma Team. With all that had happened, what started as an adventure had become a frightening struggle for survival. Holding the trash bags tightly in his left hand, Thomas moved quickly toward the light of Kevin's flashlight. The closer he got, the more clearly he could see Kevin and Joel.

"What were you doing?" Joel asked.

"Here," Thomas said, handing Joel and Kevin each one of the large black plastic trash bags. "Kevin, I need you to use your knife to cut open the sides of these bags."

Joel was still puzzled. Holding up his bag, he said, "What are these for?"

"We're going to cover ourselves up

and blend in with the darkness," Thomas said with confidence. Kevin slit the sides of the other two trash bags with his survival knife. Thomas and Joel took their cut trash bags from Kevin. They were now sheets of black plastic two feet wide and about five feet long—plenty big to cover the boys from head to foot.

Thomas led the trio to a spot about twenty feet from the side passageway. "Lay down tight against the wall, and cover yourself up with the plastic. I'll run down to the passage and see how easy it is to see you."

Kevin and Joel laid down on the damp rocky floor of the tunnel, pushing themselves tightly against the brick tunnel wall. They were already trembling with fear. The cold dampness of the tunnel just made them tremble even more. They did the best job they could of covering themselves with the sheets of plastic as Thomas took his place by the side entrance to the tunnel. Kevin and Joel had no way of seeing it, but Thomas broke into a big smile.

Kevin and Joel heard the crunch of Thomas' shoes as he ran back toward them. "Guys," Thomas called out as Joel and Kevin peeked out from behind the plastic. "The plastic makes you totally invisible! There's no way they will spot us when they get back." Just the reminder that those two men were coming back gave the boys a renewed sense of urgency about hiding themselves.

Thomas joined them, sliding himself up against the cold, damp wall and onto the rough gravel floor. All three boys pulled the plastic over themselves, each one hoping his "cloak of invisibility" would hide him from the men as well as it had hidden them from Thomas' view.

Kevin cut off his flashlight, and, for the first time, the boys were in the total darkness of the underground tunnel. It was the darkest dark they had ever experienced. To keep the darkness from swallowing them completely, they whispered to one another as they waited.

"Thomas, what did you do with those flashlights?" Joel asked his brother.

Thomas explained, "Well, do you remember that story "Hansel and Gretel," where the boy leaves the trail of breadcrumbs in the woods? I left those men a trail to follow."

"What kind of trail?" Kevin whispered.

"I left one flashlight right outside of the plastic room, near where we were tied up, shining toward the doorway. Then I put the other one behind the pile of building supplies, shining so they could see it if they looked out of the back.

Maybe, when they see we're not there, they'll go running out the back door, and look for us where the flashlight is, instead of looking for us this way."

"Cool! So they'll be going away from us instead of toward us! Good plan," Joel said to his brother. It wasn't often that Joel was impressed with Thomas' cleverness. Even though he was wrapped in fear, in darkness, and in a damp cold that had him shivering, Thomas smiled.

The boys didn't have to shiver long before they heard the metallic noises of the steel doors being opened. The two men were back. The boys could hear their muffled conversation as they got closer and closer to the place where the side passage connected to the tunnel. Thomas, Joel, and Kevin did a quick double-check to make sure their black plastic camouflage was still covering them completely.

When the men stepped into the tunnel, they were far enough from the noise of the generator that the boys could hear their conversation clearly. They had heard enough already that they knew each man by his voice. The shorter man said, "It's not like we have to shoot them or something. We just give them some bottles of water with the drugs in them, and they'll never feel a thing. Then we just dump their bodies several miles away where someone will find them quickly and we can get back to business as usual."

"A drug overdose? I can't do that. They're just kids!" said the taller man.

"You'd rather shoot them? What's your brilliant idea then? You know this is all your fault for leaving those doors unlocked," the short man said.

"What if we just scared them real bad? We could tell them that, if they tell on us, we'll come after them," the taller man argued.

The boys were taking in every word, but they were also worried that the longer these men stood there, the greater the chances that they would notice three black plastic lumps along the wall of the tunnel to their right.

"Really? Are you going to trust a bunch of kids to keep quiet about all of this? The boss has spent all that money digging the entrance, setting things up, growing these plants, finding drug dealers who will sell the final product..." The shorter man looked at his partner with frustration. "And we're just getting started here. He wants to turn the whole tunnel into a giant underground greenhouse. We're talking hundreds of millions of dollars a year, and you're worried about three kids? ...three boys who were *trespassing* by the way!"

"I *can't*, Mitch," the taller man said.

Mitch—it was the first name the boys had heard. It was a name they would never forget.

"Shut up, idiot. Let's go check on the brats and we can figure this out later. We've got a little time," the shorter man, the man named Mitch, said to his partner.

The two men walked toward the light of the plastic room. Stepping through the wall of plastic, seeing nothing where there was supposed to be three tied-up boys, the two men ran to the far end of the room, the rapid crunching of their steps telling the boys what was happening inside the glowing plastic.

Kevin whispered loudly, "Let's go!" All three boys threw off the plastic covers, rolled off of their sharp gravel beds, got on their feet and moved quickly but quietly toward the passageway that led out.

"Out here!" they heard the taller man yell from the back of the underground greenhouse. It appeared that the trail of flashlights had led them, at least for the moment, in the opposite direction.

The passageway was lit by the string of lights along the wall, so the loss of two flashlights didn't slow the boys down as they ran faster and faster for the steel doors that led to the outside. Running up the stairs, they found the doors closed. Fearing the worst—that the door was somehow locked again—all three boys pushed hard on the door. The door flew open easily, slamming loudly against the frame.

"Hey! Stop right there!" The two men had quickly discovered their deception with the flashlights and had run toward the exit to block them in, but not fast enough. They were at the far end of the passageway when they heard the door slam open. But their yell didn't slow the boys down. It had the opposite effect. All three boys ran as fast as their legs would carry them, but they still felt as if their legs were moving too slow.

When they reached the top of the hill, Joel said, "Wait, I'm going to lock them in." He turned to scramble back down the hill, but before he even got started, one of the men emerged from the doorway, and spotted the boys at the top of the hill. Joel's feet began moving in reverse, digging into the hillside and moving him backward.

Kevin and Thomas grabbed Joel's arms and dragged him backward to the top of the hill. Then all three turned and flew through the woods with briars tearing at their clothes, vines grabbing at their feet, and branches slapping them in the face. Behind them they heard the sound of yelling. They could hear footsteps in pursuit of them. They heard the engine of the truck start up and the sound of spinning tires and breaking tree limbs. The truck was bumping and weaving and crashing through the woods in pursuit of these three escaped prisoners.

CHAPTER 13: A SURPRISE ALLY

The boys were breathing so hard and running so fast that they could barely hear the sound of the truck pursuing them. But every so often the sound of a small tree trunk snapping or of the truck's spinning tires throwing rocks against the metal of the truck body rose above the noise of their gasps for air. They had run back in the same direction they had come from that morning, but they had no idea if they were still on the same path. The fear of getting lost in the woods hadn't crossed their minds. Their only thought was getting far away from the men behind them as fast as they could, whatever direction was necessary.

Just as the boys sensed that the man who was chasing them on foot was getting closer, they heard a crash and the truck's horn started blaring non-stop. They glanced at one another acknowledging that they all heard the sound, but it didn't slow down their feet.

A minute later, they emerged from the woods onto a sloping dirt and gravel road. All three boys came to a sudden stop. "Which way do we go?" Kevin asked.

Looking to the right, Joel thought he could see the road open up to a clearing. "This way," he shouted as he took off running down the hill. Kevin and Thomas followed. All three boys could feel their tired legs getting wobbly beneath them as they ran down the hill toward the clearing. The loose gravel caused them to slip and slide as they ran, draining even more of their energy.

When they cleared the trees, Joel and Thomas stopped in their tracks. Kevin stopped right behind them. They were on the road leading into the wild man's farm, and his house was just ahead. This road was his driveway. The place where they had crossed his cow pasture earlier that morning was on the opposite side of the farm, beyond the house, beyond the old barn with the rusty roof. The man's truck was parked by the house and smoke curled out of the chimney. The only way home they knew would take them a few feet from the door of the scary bearded man who lived there.

The boys looked at one another in silence. The question was so obvious that none of them had to ask it. "We've got danger behind us, and danger in front of us. What do we do?" They scanned the surrounding woods. The thought of running through more briars, brush, and vines with no idea where they might end up didn't seem like a good idea either.

Joel looked at Thomas and Kevin. "Ready?" he asked. They both knew what he meant. They would have to make a run for it across the farm to get back on the path to Kevin's house. Just then they heard the noise of two men crashing out of the woods behind them. They looked up the road just in time to see the taller man point their way and yell, "There they are!"

The boys hesitated just long enough to see the men start running in their direction. Then they took off down the driveway toward the wild man's house, running past the truck, past the door of the house, and toward the old barn. Glancing back, the boys saw the taller man getting closer. His long legs moved him faster than the boys' legs. They knew they would never make it to the other side of the pasture before the man would catch at least one of them. All three boys knew that they needed a new plan.

"This way!" Joel yelled, and he cut around the side of the barn and through the barn door. He was hoping that there might be a hiding place, a weapon, a horse saddled and ready to ride to safety... Joel had no idea how the barn would help them, but it was the only option he could see for dealing with the men who were after them.

In the barn there was an old wooden ladder to a hay loft. The boys instinctively scrambled up the ladder, but it was Kevin who immediately thought to pull the ladder up behind them, just like he did with the remote control when he climbed into his tree house at home. The bottom of the ladder rose just out of reach as the taller man ran into the barn. He stood there, staring at the boys trapped in the loft ten feet above the barn floor. About fifteen seconds later, the shorter man rounded the corner and entered the barn, so out of breath that he was wheezing.

It was then that the boys noticed the shorter man had a cut on his forehead that was bleeding. He must have hit his head when the truck crashed back in the woods. But the blood wasn't the only red on his face. The man's eyes were filled with the fire of anger, and his skin was red and wet with sweat from running. "We've got them trapped," the taller man said. "But what do we do now?"

The short man said, "I'm tempted to just take 'em out right here and now." Looking around the old barn, the short man grabbed a roll of wire that was hanging on the wall. "Let's drag them down, and tie them up tight with this wire. We can steal the truck out there and drive them back to the tunnel. We'll take care of them there."

The tall man began collecting things from inside the barn—a couple of wooden crates, a five-gallon paint bucket, a dusty old wooden chair, a scrap of plywood, and some old hay bales. Thomas, Joel, and Kevin slid as far back into the hay loft as they could while the tall man worked to stack the items high enough to get him into the loft.

Looking high on the wall behind them, Thomas noticed a bolt that connected a cable to the side of the barn. Remembering the times he and Joel had spied on the property, he remembered that this cable connected to the side of the house. It was probably the cable that supported an electric line to the barn.

Thomas knew anything was better than letting these two men capture them again, so he ran his hands through the loose straw in the loft looking for something hard. He found a metal rod about ten inches long, and used it to bang on that bolt, hoping the sound would carry across the rod into the house. It was a desperate move, but worth a try.

The taller man made his first attempt at crawling into the loft. Thomas reacted by throwing the piece of metal at the man's face. The man ducked out of the way, but it sent him tumbling down the pile of stacked items.

Kevin motioned toward the ladder and whispered to his friends, "Grab hold! If he gets up here again, maybe we can knock him down with the ladder."

The three boys gripped the ladder so tightly their knuckles turned white. As the taller man started climbing his makeshift stairs again, the shorter man called up to them, "Why don't you boys just come on down here and save us some trouble. If you cooperate, we'll be a lot nicer to you. We will get you, you know. You boys got nowhere to go!"

Another man spoke loudly, "Now what do you want with them boys?" Suddenly the barn went silent. It wasn't a voice the boys recognized. They leaned forward to see the taller man frozen motionless halfway up his homemade stairs. The shorter man's red face was now as white as a ghost. And in the doorway of the barn stood the wild man. His long, gray beard and frizzy hair were waving slightly in the breeze that blew by the doorway. His wild eyes were narrowed into a squint. In his weathered hands he held a double-barreled shotgun, pointed toward the two men, while his finger rested on the trigger.

The wild man's voice got a little louder and more intense, "Are you fellas deaf, or are you just wastin' my time? I asked you what you want with these here boys!"

The short man spoke up, "Take it easy, friend. These boys just messed with our property. We were only trying to scare them. I'm sure they've learned their lesson, so we'll just leave now. It's all good. No problem, right?"

"I think maybe you fellas should just stay right here with me for a while. I just love having visitors." The wild man spoke slowly and clearly, and his expression was deadly serious. The shotgun in his hands didn't waver. Without shifting his gaze he said to the taller man, "I see you found a couple of my chairs. Put them against the wall and you two fellas can take a seat."

The taller man slowly pulled the

chairs out of his makeshift structure, and sat them carefully against the wall. As soon as he had the chairs in place, he turned and took a seat. The wild man raised the shotgun just a fraction toward the shorter man. "How about it, friend? Don't you want to be a polite visitor and take a seat? Rude people make me jumpy. You wouldn't want to make me jumpy would you?"

The short man stepped sideways toward the wall, and moved backward into the seat. "Listen, I think this is just a big misunderstanding. We don't mean any disrespect, and we didn't mean to frighten the boys. And we're sorry for barging onto your property like this. Besides, it's getting late and we're wasting your time. So we'll just slip on out..." The short man leaned slightly forward, as if preparing to stand up.

With a tone so low it sounded like

rolling thunder, the wild man growled, "You're about to make your last mistake."

Slowly the short man sat back in his seat. Without taking his eyes off of the two men, the wild man shouted to the boys, "You two boys are Preacher Mason's sons, aren't you?"

Joel and Thomas crept forward to the edge of the hay loft. "Yes sir," Thomas said, amazed that the wild man knew who they were.

"Who's your friend?" the wild man asked.

"Kevin Freeman," Kevin said.

"Freeman, huh? You got a mighty nice treehouse, Kevin Freeman."

Kevin was amazed that this white-haired old stranger knew anything about him.

"Your father asked me to run the underground electric cable. Never seen a treehouse that fancy." After a short pause, he said, "Now you boys set the ladder down and climb down. The door is open at my house, and the phone is on the wall. Call 911 and tell them to send the police out here right away."

The boys slid the ladder back into place, and came down one at a time, with their legs still trembling in fear. Just being that close to the men who had tied them up, threatened them, and chased them had their hearts pounding in their chest. They scurried out of the barn and over to the house to place that 911 call.

It seemed to take forever for the police to arrive, though it was actually just a little over five minutes. The boys hid out behind the door of the wild man's house while he sat guard over the two men in the barn with his shotgun still leveled at them. When the policemen entered the barn, the wild man lowered his shotgun and said, "Evening, officers!

I've got a couple of gents here that you need to take away from here. I don't know the whole story, but these two were planning to hurt the boys who are waiting in my house. You'll want to talk to them to see what's really going on."

Evening was approaching and the blue flashing lights of the police car lit up the side of the wild man's house as the policemen placed the two men in handcuffs and sat them in the back seat of the police car. Then the policemen sat the three boys down and got the whole story from them. They heard about the steel doors into the tunnel, the plants growing underground, being tied up by the two men with cable ties, hearing them talk about getting rid of them, and the mention of a "boss." Thomas, Joel, and Kevin took turns explaining how they got away, about being chased, and ending up here on the farm of the man they now knew was Mr. Frasier, *Jack* Frasier.

As the investigation progressed, the DEA—Drug Enforcement Agency— arrived on the scene. These two men who had been chasing the boys were part of an operation growing plants for illegal drug distribution. This was just one part of a large criminal network on the East Coast. Questioning the two men led the DEA agents to the arrest of several people higher up in the illegal organization. While some of the agents handled the criminals, others were busy destroying all of the plants they had been growing in their secret underground greenhouse.

When the Masons and Freemans learned what their boys had been doing, the dangers they had gotten mixed up in, and how Mr. Frasier had saved them, they hugged their boys and gave them several lectures about making more responsible choices. Mr. and Mrs. Freeman and Mr. and Mrs. Mason also kept their boys on a very short leash for several months, keeping track of everywhere they went and what they were doing every minute of the day.

CHAPTER 14: BACK TO A NEW NORMAL

Monday morning, the whole story was on the front page of the local paper, with pictures of Joel, Thomas, and Kevin, the agents exiting the tunnel with the illegal plants, and how the criminals had turned the old train tunnel into their secret underground greenhouse.

As the school bus carrying Kevin, Joel, and Thomas pulled into the bus loop on Monday morning, the whole school was gathered on the sidewalk. The three boys, who secretly called themselves

Gamma Team, were greeted as heroes for helping to expose these dangerous criminals operating in their usually quiet community.

Janice and Sherry were near the front of the crowd. The two girls didn't realize it, but they were a little upset about Thomas and Joel now being local celebrities, because it meant they had to share them with even more people.

As Thomas and Joel entered the classroom, their teacher, Ms. Cox, called on her class to calm down. "Class, it's exciting to have a couple of heroes among us, but we still have plenty of work to do. We are still working on our class project about the Crozet Tunnel, but I'm going to ask Joel and Thomas if they will let us interview them later today about what they saw when they were in the tunnel this weekend. But remember, I want your questions to be about the tunnel, not the other things that happened."

As Thomas and Joel took their seats, Thomas found a note on his desk. "I'm really glad you're safe. I'm proud of you." There were some red hearts drawn at the bottom of the note, and it was signed "Jackie." Thomas looked over at Jackie and saw her smile at him. An uncontrollable smile formed on his face in response. "Wackie" didn't seem to fit as a nickname for Jackie anymore. Jackie was... *cute*! Wow, where did that come from?

When Joel and Thomas got home that evening, there were several extra places set at the table for supper. The boys learned that Mr. and Mrs. Mason had invited the Freeman family and Jack Frasier, who wasn't a "wild man" after all. Thomas and Joel enjoyed showing

Kevin their rooms, though they didn't think they had anything to show him that was as cool as Kevin's model airplanes and his amazing treehouse fortress.

At supper both families learned a lot about Mr. Frasier. He had lived in Crozet all of his life, and the farm he lived on was the same farm he grew up on. For years he worked as a truck driver for a local company, but now he was semi-retired. He kept a few cows on the farm and grew a small garden. His wife had died several years earlier and his son lived in Richmond, Virginia. He usually had a very stern look on his face, but when he was among friends he had a friendly smile and told some wonderful stories about funny things that had happened to him over the years.

Mr. Mason said to Jack Frasier, "Mr. Frasier, we will never be able to thank you enough for rescuing our children from those men. How did you know they were all out there in your barn?"

"Well, funny thing," Mr. Frasier said. "I was sittin' in my kitchen when I heard this strange noise vibrating through my whole house. I still got no idea what it was. But when I went outside to look around, I heard them men talkin' to your boys, trying to get to them. And I could tell them fellas was up to no good. So I went and got my shotgun and then I introduced myself to 'em."

Thomas didn't say a word, but he remembered beating on the bolt that connected to the cable between the barn and the house. Maybe that was what Mr. Frasier heard! Maybe that stuff they learned about sound traveling different ways had saved their lives!

Even though Mr. and Mrs. Mason and Mr. and Mrs. Freeman were all restricting where the boys were allowed to go, they gave them permission to visit Mr. Frasier's farm regularly. And old Jack Frasier was all too happy to have the company and the help of three grateful and energetic boys to help with some chores around the farm.

* * * * *

Thomas and Joel had some follow-up meetings with the police. When they saw all of the pictures the police had taken inside the tunnel as part of the investigation, they asked if they could get copies for their school report. They had several well-lit pictures of the tunnel's walls and ceiling, and gravel floor. It didn't surprise anyone that Joel and Thomas got a perfect score—100 points— on their train tunnel project. The pictures were a nice extra, but their teacher, Ms. Cox, was most impressed by the interview they did with Mr. Carter out on his farm as he told about the days when the tunnel was still in use.

The local historical society took advantage of the opportunity to do their own examination and photography in the long-abandoned tunnel. Then local authorities filled in the access passage and sealed the tunnel back up for everyone's safety.

In their final meeting with the police, the officer interviewing the boys said, "Boys, I have one last question." He laid a plastic bag on the table. The bag had the word "EVIDENCE" printed on it, with date, location, and case number written on it with a permanent marker. "I know you boys said you didn't go back any farther than just past the generator, but we found this at the very end of the tunnel. Do you know anything about this?" Inside the bag was a single walkie-talkie with rubber bands around the middle, and a short piece of fishing line tied to it. On the back, written in black marker was a name: Thomas.

ABOUT THE AUTHOR

Alan Carter Thompson is a native of Richmond, Virginia who spent 20 years in the Crozet community as the pastor of one of the local churches. He and his wife have three children who grew up there, attending the local schools and having many an adventure in the rolling hills and mountain views of the Crozet area.

Mr. Thompson was fascinated by the story of Claudius Crozet and the amazing engineering feat of the four train tunnels he designed and oversaw. The first time he saw the sealed entrance on the east end of the tunnels, he began imagining possibilities for that long, empty space in the mountain. Some of those thoughts led to this story.

The author can be reached by emailing to:

Alan.Carter.Thompson@gmail.com

Train tunnel cover art by Delaney Moje Swift, a Charlottesville native and graduate of Western Albemarle High School in Crozet, Virginia.

Isaiah 38-43   Read this

Made in the USA
Columbia, SC
29 December 2020

28657333R00104